KINGDOM OF LIGHT

Shatter the Darkness

J. H. Lee

Contents

Dedication ↓ larger font

Page 4

1 - The Living Dead

As for you, you were dead in your transgressions and sins,
In which you used to live when you followed the ways of this world and
Of the ruler of the kingdom of the air...
(Book of Truth - Ephesians 2:1,2)

The Land of the Dead. The Kingdom of Darkness.

That was my home, my land, and my country. It was where my citizenship was, and as a resident of that place, I was known as the "Dead" or the "Living Dead." The ruler of that land called himself the Prince of Darkness for his whole kingdom was cloaked with a blanket of grey.

As a native of his kingdom, I was obedient to the laws of the land, for the Prince and his army Hordes were ruthless. They were cruel taskmasters, organized and divided into troops of regiments. They ruled through the power of fear. They did not treat me as a free citizen. I was regarded as a slave, bound in chains.

And yet, as strange as it may sound, I did not entirely hate my time spent in that place, for that kingdom offered pleasures and amusements that I whole-heartedly took part in.

The Slop Pits were my favorite place to hang out. When the wind was just right, the aroma of those pits tickled the hairs of my nose with pure delight and captured my attention. I could not resist the smell. I would abandon whatever I was doing, race towards them, and jump in whole-heartedly, immersing myself in the rottenness of decaying matter. I craved the reckless, wild living for when I was distracted by it, I could almost forget my chains and the truth of who I was and what my future entailed. I was nothing more than a slave and as such my final destiny would lead me through the Gates of Death.

I had never traveled through the Gates of Death. The ones who did never returned to tell us what was on the other side. A high wall separated the Kingdom of Darkness from the Land of No Return, which lay beyond the gates. A putrid and horrendous scent cloaked with a dense, grey smoke continually clung to the air above the gates. Black Scavengers – black vultures skilled in the art of skinning and devouring the flesh of slaves – patrolled the wall. It seemed they were forever squawking and never silent – except when the Gates of Death opened.

When the gates opened, they hovered in the air, their eyes burning with greed as they prepared to shred and feast on the one who had been chosen to go from Darkness to Death. When the gates closed, the silence ended as they descended like a black moth, with their talons extended. Their screeches mingled with the cries of despair, pain, and anguish.

I never saw what happened behind the wall, but I knew that one day I would, for that was the final destination of every citizen of the Kingdom of Darkness. We did not know when the call of death would come, but each of us understood that one day we would be chosen to go through the Gates of Death. Never to return.

On some days, when I stood in just the right place, echoes of the continual, anguishing screams could be heard from those who now resided in the Land of No Return. I remember the first time I overheard those cries and realized that going through the Gates of Death did not mean a person stopped existing. While the flesh of those who went through the gates was devoured by the Scavengers of Death, there was a part of ~~them~~ *the person* that lived on, suffering continually.

And so, I lived in the Kingdom of Darkness, giving myself over to any whim and gratifying any desire that I thought of, *as I tried* ~~trying~~ to forget my destiny. When I could not ignore the truth of my end, I attempted to live a good life in hopes that I could alter my future. But at the end of each day, my fate was unchanged. I was still in chains.

2 – The Slave Market

For the wages of sin is death...
(Book of Truth - Romans 6:23)

Now within the Kingdom ~~Land~~ of Darkness, there was a place known as the Slave Market. On any given moment – day or night – slaves were sold, ~~but~~ there was only one purchaser, a buyer named Death.

Any slave that was to be purchased by Death had the opportunity to attempt to buy his or her freedom and life by paying the sin debt he or she owed. As the slave was brought before a set of scales, the weight of each one's sin was placed on one plate of the scale. Immediately, the empty plate on the other side lifted into the air.

It was onto this raised plate that a slave could place whatever he or she felt should be able to balance the debt owing. If the scales became even, the slave would be set free and would gain life. If the scales remained uneven, the slave would be handed over to Death, who - like a greedy vulture – would snatch and drag each slave to the Gates of Death. Once there, he would command the gates to open inwards and receive the slave he hurled into the Land of No Return. As the gates shut, the Scavengers of Death descended to feast on the flesh of the now departed slave.

No amount of pleading, begging, or fighting could stop the inevitable. When Death came to claim a slave, time was up.

I remember one day with crystal clear recollection. Usually the Slave Market was a place that each citizen avoided; however, on that day, I was drawn to sit and watch. I hid among a pile of rocks and tried to not be seen. I looked at the slaves who had been rounded up for that day by the Hordes. From this group, Death chose whichever ones he wanted. I do not know what drove his decisions.

That day, a handsome man, with steely eyes and a healthy body was chosen. As he swaggered to the scale, he flexed his bulging muscles. Strength rippled as one muscle after another was stretched and loosened. Confidently, he placed one arm on the scale and pushed down. Nothing happened.

Next, he pressed down with two hands. By this time, the confident smirk left, and sweat was beginning to glisten on his forehead. The scale did not budge. He took a few steps back, leaped into the air and tried to shove the scale to the ground with all his might. Again, nothing happened. Death's cavernous mouth opened as a mocking laugh erupted. His talons clamped down on the arm of the now quivering slave. The slave dug in his feet as he struggled to break free, but all his strength could not overcome the grip of Death. The Gates of Death opened, and the man was flung inside.

The next slave chosen was a silver-haired man with clothes of the most beautiful cloth. Rings of gold and precious gems decorated his fingers, and he held in his arms a box. He set the elaborately decorated chest on the ground in front of the scale and opened it. It contained blocks of pure gold for he was a very wealthy man. He placed one brick on the scale, but nothing happened.

He added another and another until finally the last brick was placed. The balance on the scales had not moved. Frantically, he checked the box one last time, as if hoping to find what was not there. He glanced at his hands, pulled off the rings and added them to the pile of gold.

I remember watching his eyes dart back and forth from one side of the scale to the other – as if he was hoping to see a flicker of movement. There was none. His head dropped in shame as he realized that his wealth was not enough to buy his freedom. He was led away by Death and the gates opened inward as he was flung through them. I never saw him again.

Another slave was brought forward. This woman carried with her many ledgers were inscribed with the words "Good Deeds of My Life." She placed one ledger on the scale. Nothing changed. She added another and another. Finally, every journal had been set on the scale. I watched, as in desperation, she searched the ground for any that might have fallen, but she did not find any.

Even though she had performed many good works while living, they were not enough to remove the debt owing against her. She cried out in despair as she was handed over to Death. The doors opened inwards, and she was pushed through. The scavengers descended. Within seconds they returned to their perch on the wall, squawking, screeching, and waiting for another victim.

The next one chosen by Death was a young person, not yet old. I remember him because he carelessly swaggered up to the scales. He tossed a rock onto the balance, and said, "Open the gates. All my friends are there. I am going to join them and party it up."

Horrified at his recklessness, I nearly cried out, "You fool! Don't you know what is beyond those gates?"

He was led to the gates and pushed through. The birds of prey descended. I had to cover my ears against the sheer despair of the cries that I heard. Those were not sounds of a joyous reunion. Instead, they were cries of fear, misery, and terrible anguish.

I watched that day as people of all types – those with beauty, strength, wealth, intelligence, humor, and goodness – were chosen to be handed over to Death. Each one brought forward what they had counted on to save them, yet no one could budge the scales. The debt of sin was too big, and every single one of those people went through the Gates of Death.

Finally, I could bear it no longer. I had to get out of that place, so I got up and made my way to a solitary outcropping of rocks. I huddled against the cold stone and thought about the debt that I owed. I had nothing of value to pay it. I pulled my knees up to my chest as hopelessness descended. Misery filled my heart and tears of anguished frustration trailed down my cheeks, for my end would be the same as that of the victims I saw this day.

And I was unable to stop it or change it.

3 - An Ember of Hope

... "Why do you look for the living among the dead?
He is not here; he has risen!"
(Book of Truth - Luke 24:5)

Later that night I awakened. As I stretched my cold and stiff joints, I noticed an eerie, flickering light that tinged the air orange around me. I glanced around the corner of the outcropping, and there on the other side of the rock, clustered around a fire, huddled soldiers of the Horde. I could see in the distance a few of the prisoners they had captured for the next day's Slave Market. Quietly I slunk back against the wall, trying desperately not to be seen or heard. I did not want to get their attention.

While I remained hidden, their low voices reached my ears, and I listened to their conversation. It was a story that caught my attention.

"Have the Gates of Death ever opened out?" a high pitched voice asked.

"Out?" responded another.

"Yes, out," the questioner probed. "The gates seem to only open inwards. Everybody goes in, but nobody comes out. Has anyone ever come out?"

Curious, I sat up straighter. As far as I knew, the Gates of Death had never opened out. For that to happen, someone would have to go in, die, and then come back to life to walk out. It seemed impossible. Unimaginable. I found myself listening intently, for if such an event had happened, it could only mean one thing!

The Prince of Darkness and Death had been overpowered, defeated and crushed by a strength stronger than they. I leaned forward as a rough voice, rusty from no use, grated the air.

"There was one time when the inward force of the Gates of Death was reversed, and they opened outward." He paused for a moment and coughed. Silence hung in the air until he spoke again. "The Prince does not like to acknowledge it and tries to keep all record of it hidden. But if one were to go to the right-hand side of the Gates of Death, an account would be found of the time the doors opened outward."

"Who was it?" squeaked the inquirer.

"It was a Lamb. I remember the day well, for the Lamb did not resemble any of the slaves that came to the Slave Market. He was spotless and clean. The light that came from him shattered the darkness that surrounded us."

"As well, he was not dragged to the Slave Market as every other slave is. The Lamb walked up to the auction block on his own. Although he owed no debt, he bound himself with chains and placed the weight of everyone's sin on himself. The Prince of Darkness grabbed hold of the chains and led the Lamb to the Gates of Death. The Hordes flogged and beat him along the way until his body was no longer spotless and clean. It was red, as blood flowed from it. When he reached the Gates of Death, they opened inward, and Death hurled the Lamb inside. As soon as the doors close, the Prince of Darkness called for a party, and what a time of revelry it was. It lasted for three days, and may have gone on forever, if only…"

The speaker paused for a long moment.

"What happened?"

The voice coughed again and continued. "There was an earthquake that shook the foundations of the Kingdom. The Prince looked at the Gates of Death. They shuddered for a moment and then exploded outwards as the Lamb walked out. He was as white as snow and light glowed from his coat. He walked up to the balance of scales and stepped onto the empty side. With one foot the balance quivered. With two feet it began to move. With the third foot, it was in balance, and with the fourth foot the weight of the debt catapulted off the balance. There was no debt owing. He had conquered sin. He had conquered Death. He had conquered the Prince of Darkness. He alone was almighty."

Unknowingly, I had moved towards the fire during the discourse. When it was done, I huddled back into my hiding place as I took in all I heard. At one time, the Gates of Death opened outward? Their normal movement had been reversed by a Lamb more powerful than the Prince of Darkness? That night, as I contemplated these things, an ember of hope began to flicker in my soul.

4 - The Discovery

Ask and it will be given to you;
Seek and you will find;
Knock and the door will be opened to you.
(Book of Truth - Matthew 7:7)

The next day, instead of reveling in the Slop Pits, I turned my attention towards the Gates of Death. With the story of the night before clinging to my mind, I tried to recall and understand what I heard. Was it possible? Could the gates have opened outward?

I walked past the Slave Market, and the Hordes did not stop me. The Scavengers of Death flew past me and flapped their wings in my face, but they seemed to know that I was not part of their meal for that day. Finally, I stood before the Gates of Death. They loomed high above me, towering to an elevation that could not be scaled.

On the left side, under the title of "Those Who Have Went In" was a record of all the slaves who had entered the gates. The names were endless. The Prince of Darkness left the names there as part of his reign of terror. The list served to remind his subjects of their eternal destiny. It took only one look for the image of the listing of names to be branded on our minds and for us to be haunted with the knowledge that one day those stones would bear our names.

But today, I focused my attention on the right-hand side, searching for the evidence that what I had heard the night before was true. If the Lamb had come out of the Gates of Death, his name should be recorded. I walked up to the grey walls and gazed at the lettering I found there. Its appearance glowed as I read the words "Those Who Have Come Out." Underneath two words were recorded.

The Lamb.

Stunned, I backed up. It was true. The Gates had opened out. There was someone stronger and more powerful than Death and the Prince of Darkness. That someone was called the Lamb.

If this half of the story was real, then the other half must also be correct. That part had told of how the Lamb stepped on the scale and flung the weight of sin into the air. I reasoned that if the Gates of Death could not contain the Lamb, then the debt of sin could be removed when the Lamb stepped onto the scales.

I walked past the Slave Market and watched as person after person tried to remove their debt and balance the scales. Nothing worked, and one by one they were forced through the Gates of Death.

As I left that place, I considered my destiny. There was nothing I could do to save myself. I was not good enough, rich enough, smart enough, pretty enough, strong enough, or talented enough to remove my debt.

Yet, the Lamb was able to do away with the weight of the debt. Could it happen again? If I could find him, perhaps he would help me. Maybe he would tell me what to do so that my destiny changed.

And I could be set free.

5 - The Search

For everyone who asks receives;
The one who seeks finds; and
To the one who knocks, the door will be opened.
(Book of Truth - Matthew 7:8)

Walking throughout the Kingdom of Darkness, I began to search for the Lamb.

And you know what?

As soon as I started to seek him, I found him! He was standing by a narrow, wooden gate that I often traveled by on my way to the Slop Pits. Even though I had passed that spot many times, I did not recall seeing him there. My eyes had been blind to him, yet once I became aware of his presence, I could not forget him.

The greyness that shrouded everything in the Kingdom of Darkness did not cloak him. Instead, from him radiated a glow – a light – that shattered the darkness and caused it to flee. It was in the brightness of himself that I made another discovery about the Lamb.

Chains did not bind him as I was bound. He was free.

A longing to be liberated from my chains erupted in me. Could the Lamb break my shackles? I took a step towards him, but when he looked at me, I felt dirty and unworthy. So, I bolted from the Lamb and ran to the Slop Pit. There I jumped in and joined my friends in the carousing, but I could not give myself over to the reckless, wild living as enthusiastically as I once had.

Wherever I went, I could not forget the eyes of the Lamb. Although in his presence I had felt the dirtiness of myself, there was also something else in his gaze that drew me. He was not the one who pushed me away. I was the one who had run away. Could it be that he wanted me to come to him? Was he calling me to come?

When I returned to the narrow gate, there the Lamb stood. Waiting. For me.

This time, instead of running away, I took a step closer and looked into his eyes. They were unlike anything I had seen before. Light – pure and brilliant – flowed from them that pierced through the darkness and saw straight to my heart.

6 - The Light

The eye is the lamp of the body…
…If then the light within you is darkness,
How great is that darkness!
(Book of Truth - Matthew 6:22, 23)

Now you may wonder, why I thought that the light coming out of the eyes of the Lamb was so different. It can be difficult to explain, but I will try. You see, each citizen in the Kingdom of Darkness had eyes, but the light that came from our eyes was darkness.

Sound confusing?

Think of wearing sunglasses on a bright, sunny day. The sunglasses are designed to keep out the light. In our case, the darkness in our eyes allowed us to see in the Kingdom of Darkness. I could easily find my way to the Slop Pits every day, and I could travel throughout the kingdom. But, at the same time, the darkness of my eyes was designed to keep me blind and unable to see the light of the Lamb.

It was not until I saw the eyes of the Lamb that I even noticed a difference. At first, I wanted to run and hide, for the light coming from his eyes exposed the darkness that was in me. Think of how a flashlight works in a darkened room. That light not only brightens up the whole area, but it also exposes all the things that had been kept hidden by the darkness.

In other words, everything exposed by the light became visible. When the eyes of the Lamb shone on me, I saw who I was.

In his light, I saw for the first time that my clothes were rags and full of holes. Not only that, but I also noticed movement under the fabric. I pulled back the ratted sleeve of my shirt and was horrified to see my skin crawling with masses of white, wriggling maggots that covered black, rotting flesh. Without the light of the Lamb, I would have never seen the rottenness and decay. I was full of darkness.

With these new findings, my brain felt like a quickly expanding balloon that was about to burst. I shrank back from the light of the Lamb and tried to hide behind a rock as a horrible realization crept into my mind.

I was already dead. A rotting corpse. How could I not have known it before?

My mind went back to the day I had watched the Slave Market where citizen upon citizen had presented riches, intelligence, beauty, popularity, goodness, and so many other things in an attempt to remove the weight of sin, but each one had failed.

As I cowered behind the rock, frantically trying to scratch the squirming maggots off my skin, I realized why the citizens of the Kingdom of Darkness could not save themselves. How can people already dead overpower Death? Was it possible that the Lamb had defeated death because he was life itself?

I huddled in the shadows of the rock as the brilliance of the Lamb kept filling the darkness. Now I understood why the Prince of Darkness kept us blind to the light of the Lamb. Surely if we saw and knew the uselessness of using our strategies to try to remove the debt of sin and escape Death, we would stop trying to use our own strategies, and seek aid from the one who could help us.

By hiding the truth of our condition while allowing us to devise ways to save ourselves as we pursued the pleasures of the Kingdom of Darkness, we would never know our real state. The fact that we were dead already proved that death was stronger than us. As people already dead, our eternal destiny could only lead through the Gates of Death.

And that would be the end, for no one going through those gates ever came back.

Except for the Lamb.

I peeked around the rock and caught a glimpse of the only one who had come back from the Gates of Death. The fact that he was standing on the other side of the rock behind which I was hiding was proof that he was alive, and not dead. He had conquered death.

I looked down at my rotting corpse. I could not protect myself from death. I knelt on my knees and crept into the light towards the Lamb. Maybe, just maybe, he would save me.

7 – The Call

"But everything exposed by the light becomes visible…"
"For God did not send his Son into the world to condemn the world,
But to save the world through him."
(Book of Truth - Ephesians 5:13 and John 3:17)

As I crawled towards the Lamb, emotions stampeded through me. Disgust and horror of my condition. Shame at my dirtiness compared to his dazzling pureness. Awe in the understanding that the Lamb had conquered death. Hope that I may have found the answer I was looking for.

A wind blew from the east carrying with it the smell of the Slop Pits. It was then that I noticed a difference in the scent of the air that surrounded the Lamb. It was refreshing and sweet. While the stench of death clung to me, the fragrance of life surrounded him.

The nearer I drew to the Lamb, the more brilliant the light became, but instead of hiding from it, I was drawn to it. In his brightness, the holes in my ratted clothing became more apparent as the squiggling of the maggots intensified. The light infuriated them. Ignoring their frenzied attack on my rotting flesh, I continued forward. His light not only exposed the holes that covered my rotting flesh, but it also pierced to my heart and mind. He knew about the dirty thoughts and the desires that had once seemed so tantalizing and delightful to me.

Now, I regretted them.

Next, to the pure, radiant light of the Lamb, I felt dirty. Unclean. Ashamed. Incredibly, he did not chase me away – even though he saw every part of me. He did not turn his back on me, nor cast me out of his presence. He did not condemn me.

Instead, he spoke one word to me.

"Come."

8 – The Payment of Love

For God so loved the world that he gave his one and only Son,
That whoever believes in him shall not perish but have eternal life.
(Book of Truth - John 3:16)

I obeyed the command of the Lamb to come, and there I knelt before him. Never before had I been so unmasked. He saw me for who I was, and his light enabled me to see who I was. I knew that I needed help that only he could give. I had a debt of sin owing that I could not pay. With head bowed and knees bent, I humbly asked, "Can you help me?"

The Lamb did not speak, but he took me by the hand and began to lead me. Looking back, I am not sure how he took my hand, but I will never forget where he led me – straight to the Slave Market.

"No! Wait! Stop!" I cried in panic as a vice of fear squeezed my heart. The Slave Market was a place one went as willingly as one would swallow porcupine quills. Everyone I knew – and I mean everyone – avoided entering the Slave Market. Only those taken by the Hordes came here, for once one entered, it was just a few steps to the Gates of Death.

"Do you want to be free and live?"

With the accuracy of a two-edged sword, the words of the Lamb pierced my heart. Even as fear climbed into my throat and the maggots swarming over my skin squirmed viciously, the Lamb's question revealed that he knew the sincere desire of my heart. I wanted to be free. I wanted to live. I did not want to go through the Gates of Death. I looked up into his eyes and nodded.

"Then trust me," he said. "Follow me for I am the way, the truth, and the life."

Before I followed him, I had something to say. "I am sorry. I know that there is nothing that I can do to pay my debt and save myself. You are the only one who can help me."

"I forgive you," the Lamb stated simply and together we entered the Slave Market.

Everyone and everything stopped as the Lamb walked boldly to the scales. I did not feel nearly so courageous as I stood beside him and attempted to hide my panic. Behind me was the group of slaves the Hordes had rounded up for that day. The Scavengers of Death perched on their place along the wall. They preened their feathers, having just returned from feasting on their last victim. In front of me and behind the scale stood Death. The black of darkness that erupted from his eyes was overwhelming, and for a moment I felt helpless and hopeless.

I was a slave with a debt that I could not pay. Consequently, my destiny was death.

I looked to the Lamb. In his radiance, the heavy dread that had descended on me when Death speared me with his gaze, was exchanged for something I had not known or felt before. At that time I did not know what to call it, but I knew it was the opposite of the heavy weight of fear that had continuously been a part of my life until that point.

Then I heard the Lamb speak the words that changed my destiny. Forever. Addressing the Keeper of the Scales, the Lamb said, "I have come to pay the debt owing for this slave."

"What do you bring?" the Keeper of the Scales snarled as he placed the weight of my sin on the balance.

"Myself!" The Lamb boldly stepped forward. He put one foot on the balance, and the scale shuddered. He placed his second foot on, the scale creaked. With the third foot, the balance of the scale was even. With the fourth foot, my debt catapulted through the air to such a height that I could no longer see it.

The instant the weight of my debt was flung away, many events happened all at once. The Gates of Death opened inwards, but then they were thrown outwards with such force that the Scavengers of Death struggled to keep their footing on the wall. The chains that bound me shattered and I found myself positioned on the opposite side of the scale on a narrow path called Life. Fresh skin that was whole and not decomposing replaced the maggots and decaying flesh. My new, white clothes glowed with the light of the Lamb.

"How did this happen?" I asked in amazement.

"By believing in me," he said. "When I died and then came back to life, I conquered Death and the Prince of Darkness. They have no power over me. When anyone chooses to trust in me, I pay the debt owing against them and set them free."

"But, why?" I asked. Even though I was thankful for what the Lamb had done, I did not understand why he would do that for me.

He gazed at me with the same look that had drawn me to him and said three simple words.

"I love you."

I shook my head in confusion. "You paid my debt and set me free because you love me? I am not special nor have I done anything heroic. Why would you love me?"

"My love for you is not hinged on who you are, nor is it earned or lost by what you have done or not done." The Lamb had an earnest expression on his face as he continued. "I love you, and I give you my love because I have chosen to love you."

As the Lamb led me on the narrow path towards the narrow, wooden gate where I had first spotted him, his words tumbled around in my mind. His love was a constant, steadfast love that was not earned or lost by who I was or what I had done or not done.

Who had heard of a love like that?

I hadn't. Love in the Kingdom of Darkness was like a commodity that was earned, gained, traded, sold, and lost by what a person did and said...

Or by what they did not do or say.

That is what made the love of the Lamb so different. I had not done anything to earn his love. Yet, I could not deny what he said for I had experienced the truth of his choice to love me. It was because of his love for me that he had given his own life to set me free and give me life.

As I struggled to grasp this previously unknown love, I knew that I wanted to discover more about this Lamb –

And his love for me.

9 - The Narrow Gate

Enter through the narrow gate. For wide is the gate and broad is the road that leads to destruction, and many enter through it. But small is the gate and narrow is the road that leads to life, and only a few find it.
(Book of Truth - Matthew 7:13, 14)

The Lamb and I stood before the wooden gate where I first found him. As I perused the gate, its narrowness surprised me. There was only room for one person at a time – without possessions – to travel through. Entering this gate would not be a group activity.

Beyond the gate, I saw a country filled with color and life. At the sight of it, my heart began to briskly beat with eagerness. "What is that place?" I questioned.

"That is my kingdom, the Kingdom of Light," the Lamb said. "The only entrance to it is through this Narrow Gate."

"Why is the gate so narrow? Wouldn't it be easier and more convenient to have a wider gate? That way if someone wanted to bring some luggage, it would fit, or if a group of friends wanted to go, they could all travel through together."

The Lamb shook his head and gestured towards a small table that was positioned just to the left of the Narrow Gate. "A person doesn't get into my kingdom with a lot of stuff or having the right friends." He pointed to a golden book that lay on the table. "To get through the Narrow Gate, your name must be written in this book called the Book of Life."

The Lamb opened the book. Names of people filled its pages. Finally, he stopped at one page, and there I saw my name! Since my name was written in that book, I would be able to go through the Narrow Gate and enter the Kingdom of Light. Before I did that, I had to ask another question.

"What are all those other names that are in the Book of Life?"

"Those are all the people who, like you, choose to believe in me and let me pay the debt that they owe. They choose to follow my way – the way of life – and enter through my gate – the Narrow Gate – that leads to my kingdom. They are no longer citizens of the Kingdom of Darkness. They are citizens of my kingdom - the Kingdom of Light."

Thousands of pages filled the book. I wondered aloud, "Are these the names of all the people who have ever lived?"

The Lamb unlocked the Narrow Gate and stepped through, but when he looked at me, his eyes were full of sorrow. Tears spilled over and ran down his face. He shook his head, "No, it isn't. Many think that a wide gate and a broad path is easier and more convenient. Although they want life, they think that they can attain life on a wide path and through a wide gate of their own making."

"But, while a wide path and the wide gate may look like they lead to life, they don't. People who go through a wide gate will never receive eternal life, nor will they reach my kingdom. The broad path and wide gate lead to the Gates of Death. I am the way, the truth, and the life. The only way to receive eternal life and enter the Kingdom of Light is on the narrow path and through the narrow gate that I have made."

The Lamb paused, and the sorrow in his eyes turned to delight. He looked straight at me and said, "Come!"

I walked towards the gate and noticed that my steps seemed to be buoyant. As I stepped forward into my new life, I realized that this lightness I felt was because I was walking without the weight of my shackles and chains holding me down.

I was free!

Excitement erupted from the light of the Lamb's eyes as he waited for me to join him. The anticipation in his gaze seemed to indicate he had an extraordinary surprise to share with me, and his joy was contagious. Eager to see what was on the other side, I ran to the gate and stepped through.

10 - The Kingdom of Light

For he has rescued us from the dominion of darkness
And brought us into the kingdom of the Son he loves,
In whom we have redemption, the forgiveness of sins.
(Book of Truth - Colossians 1:13, 14)

As I passed through the Narrow Gate, I left the Kingdom of Darkness behind and stepped into a place flavored with a tantalizing aroma. Where the stench of death and decay had coated the air of the Kingdom of Darkness, the fragrance of life filled the atmosphere of the Lamb's kingdom.

The moment I stepped through the gate, I halted. There was so much to see and to take in, it was hard to move. The air was alive with light and filled with majestic goodness. "What did you say this place was?" I whispered in awe.

The Lamb laughed with delight, "This is the Kingdom of Light."

I took another step into this new place. It was absolutely, utterly spectacular. Instead of darkness, there was light. Instead of the stench of decay, there was an aroma of life. Instead of black and grey, the world was painted with hues of the rainbow.

The colors twinkled and sparkled in a complicated dance as they filled the space around me. Everything their graceful fingers touched seemed to burst with color unimaginable. Vibrant blues, ruby reds, glittering greens, joyful yellows, peaceful purples, and so many more that I could not even name.

As I watched the lively colors of this new kingdom dance around me full of joy, I realized that they only reflected what was taking place in my heart. Not only had I been set free from the chains that bound me but for the first time in my life, I was completely and fully alive – on the inside. A vibrant, joyful feeling filled my heart and my mind for instead of being filled with fear, dread, and terror, I had a hope that was tangible, real and living.

Yes! That's what was inside of me. A living hope! The hope I had known previously was rooted in wishful desires and feelings but resulted in disappointment when those desires were unfulfilled.

I was tasting freedom, love, and hope for the first time. As these bold truths took root in my mind and heart, the delight erupted within me. I leaped into the air and ran as fast as I could until my breath ran out. Chains no longer kept me bound.

I was free, alive, and filled to the brim with a living hope!

11 - The Lay of the Land

It shone with the glory of God,
And its brilliance was like that of a very precious jewel…
(Book of Truth - Revelation 21:11)

As I gulped in the air and filled my lungs with the sweet aroma of that kingdom, I leaped into the air and spun in joyful freedom. This was life. Abundant Life. Unbound Life. A life better and greater anything I had known. I twirled until I was dizzy, and had to stop. As my pulse returned to normal, I surveyed the kingdom of which I was now a part.

In the distance – at the horizon where the line of earth and sky meet – I beheld a stunning sight. Although that place was hidden by clouds, it radiated with such an intense, beautiful glow that the light of the Kingdom of Light seemed pale in comparison. Flashes of jeweled colors, like that of a living rainbow, peeked around the linings of the clouds. Even though the majesty of that land was veiled, the glory of that place was unable to be entirely hidden. Its brilliance that pierced through the clouds was so intense and bright I could not stare at it for long.

"What is that place?" I asked. A longing to be there filled me.

The Lamb looked in the direction my finger pointed. "That is Heaven, and it is your final home. A place is being prepared for you there."

"How quickly can I get there?" I asked, eager to get going. If I walked and ran, maybe it would not take too long.

The Lamb laughed and motioned for me to come. "Each citizen of the Kingdom of Light receives a personal summons to Heaven. Until that day, each one is given a personalized path to follow through the Kingdom of Light."

"Do I have to travel this path alone?" I questioned. Although I was thankful to be a citizen of a new land, I was not sure I wanted to venture through it alone. Everything in it was new to me.

"No, you will not be alone, for I will always be with you. I will never leave you or turn my back on you. Follow me, and I will show you the path I have prepared for you."

As I followed the Lamb, I looked over my shoulder. There, behind me, some distance away stood a row of trees that were colorless and dead. In their branches, I saw some black birds. Their hoarse croaks sent chills through me for I knew what they were.

The Scavengers of Death.

At that moment they lifted off the branches, swirling together until they appeared to be a solid mass. They hovered in the air for a moment and then descended with a flurry. Screams of their victim mingled with their course screeches.

Horrified, I shuddered as they returned to their place in the trees and pruned their feathers as they waited for their next victim. I knew that place all too well. It was the Kingdom of Darkness, yet it looked different. Something was missing.

"Where is the wall?" I asked. When I had lived in the Kingdom of Darkness, there had been a wall that surrounded the entire land.

"The wall is something that only those who are citizens in the Kingdom of Darkness can see, for it is only over them that the wall has power. The Prince of that land built the wall to keep the people there from seeing and entering into the Kingdom of Light. The only way to come into the Kingdom of Light is by the Narrow Gate that you came through."

"But how can they ever come into the Kingdom of Light if they cannot see it? Do they even know it is there?"

The Lamb considered my question and then asked, "Do you remember Sophia?"

Sophia? Sifting through my memories, I remembered an old friend who had visited me when I was in chains as a slave of the Kingdom of Darkness. I mocked her because she did not look or act like me. She was clothed in white, and she would not join me in the Slop Pits as she used to.

The Lamb continued. "I sent her to you so that you would begin to see that there was something different than just the Kingdom of Darkness."

"You sent her to me? But I didn't even know you!" I said in surprise.

The Lamb smiled. "I knew you and was calling you long before you knew me. It was after seeing her that your eyes were opened to see the inability of anyone in the Kingdom of Darkness to get rid of the debt owing against them. You began to seek for another way, and then you found me."

My mouth opened and then closed again. In my mind, I traced the events that the Lamb described. It was as he said. Even though I feared death, I had not been looking for him at all, because I was determined to live my life the way I wanted.

Until Sophia.

She had looked and acted so different. She had not responded with unkindness to the mean words and taunts that I had hurled her way. Instead, she had smiled and helped to bring relief to my skin. At her touch,

I had felt a measure of peace. When she left, the peace that radiated from her went with her. In its place, I felt something I had not known before.

Discontentment.

After that, I began to look at the Kingdom of Darkness with eyes that saw for the first time the fruitlessness and inability of anyone there to save themselves. It was when I realized how hopelessly lost I was, that I had turned to see the Lamb and hear him call me to come. When I answered his call, he paid my debt and set me free from the chains of sin and death that bound me.

At this truth, I leaped up into the air once again and laughed out loud with pure joy. What else could I do?

I was free!

12 – Loved Always…Forever…No Matter What

…"I have loved you with an everlasting love;
I have drawn you with unfailing kindness."
(Book of Truth - Jeremiah 31:3)

The Lamb joined me in laughter, and together we ran through the grass with freedom and delight. Together, we ran through the flowers, chasing after the colorful rays of light. Together, we ran until we came to the banks of a stream whose water bubbled with joy as it flowed over rocks tinted with emerald, ruby, sapphire, and gold.

I breathed deeply, once again filling my lungs with the flavorful air of that land. It was like breathing in the air that is bursting with the aroma of freshly baked cinnamon buns, the sweet smell of hot chocolate and the pleasant fragrance of strawberries.

I laughed out loud, and so did the Lamb!

As my heart rate slowed, I knelt along the river's edge and took a drink of water. My thirst quenched, I leaned back against a large rock and watched the Lamb.

Delight was radiating from his eyes as he said, "You would not believe how long I have been waiting to do that! And this!"

My left eyebrow went up. I pointed back over the field where we had been running and questioned, "That?"

The Lamb smiled. "That."

Quizzically, I sat there; both eyebrows now raised high in confusion. We were not doing anything now, except sitting together beside the river's edge.

"This?" I asked.

"This!" the Lamb repeated. Amusement filled his eyes as he turned to me and repeated, "This! Spending time with you. Laughing. Running. Delighting in you and with you as you live this life that is now yours. All this is what I have been waiting to do for a long time."

His words surprised me for in all honesty I could not remember anyone just taking pleasure in spending time with me by running and laughing with me. In the Kingdom of Darkness, when people spent time with me, it usually meant that they wanted something from me or they needed me to do something for them.

"How long have you been waiting to spend time with me?" I wondered out loud.

The Lamb paused and then said softly, "Since before the beginning of time."

My jaw dropped in utter confusion. I could not think of anything to say. What the Lamb said seemed impossible. Before the beginning of time? What did that mean? The Lamb quietly waited as I tried to process what he said.

Finally, I managed to untangle my thoughts, but where they were leading me seemed hard to understand. "If you have been waiting since before the beginning of time, that means you are...are…" I paused, unable to think of the right word.

The Lamb filled in the blank. "Eternal."

"Eternal? Like everlasting? Without beginning or end?" I questioned, but then I continued speaking without waiting for an answer. "If you've been waiting that long that means that you knew me before…before…" I paused again. The idea taking root in my mind seemed improbable.

"You are right," he said.

"What?"

"You are right," he repeated.

"But I didn't say anything!"

"Not out loud, but your thoughts are speaking much!" The Lamb chuckled and then nodded. "You are right. I knew you before you were even born."

At this point, my thoughts became a jumbled tangle as I tried to process what the Lamb was revealing about himself. He was eternal, without beginning or end. His knowledge included knowing me before I even came into being and he knew my thoughts.

The Lamb continued to watch me with an amused smile.

I opened my mouth to ask him the question that was on my lips, but before I could voice the words, he spoke.

"Yes, I am."

I sat there stunned. Again, the Lamb had spoken the answer to my question before I voiced it, verifying the truth that he was all-knowing.

I turned away from the Lamb and gazed at the stream. Its peaceful waters helped to calm the chaos that was swirling in my mind.

Who was this Lamb? He was unlike anyone that I had ever known. Slowly, I began to put together the small pieces of truth that I was learning about him.

He had been waiting to spend time with me since before the beginning of time. That meant that he was eternal.

He knew me before the beginning of time, and he knew my thoughts before I even spoke them. That meant he was all-knowing.

I remembered back to the moment that he had delivered me from my sins and rescued me from the power of Death and the Prince of Darkness. Even though their hatred for the Lamb had radiated from them, they had been powerless to stop him. That meant there was none more powerful than he.

He was all powerful. He was eternal. He was all-knowing. And he had been waiting for all eternity to spend time –

"With you." The Lamb's voice broke into my thoughts.

"Why?" I asked.

"Because I love you. Always. Forever. No matter what."

I sat quietly as his words sank into my heart and my mind. I had already experienced a small part of his love when he told me that his reason for rescuing me was not because of what I had done or who I was. Instead, he saved me because he chose to love me.

But now, I was beginning to see the magnitude of his love for me.

He loved me always. Because he was all powerful, nothing would be able to overpower or change his love for me.

He loved me forever. Because he was eternal, his love for me had no end.

He loved me no matter what. Because he was all knowing, he knew everything that I had done in the past and everything that I would do in the future, and he still chose to love me.

As I gazed into the Lamb's eyes, I found myself swallowed in an ocean of love so deep, so high, so wide and so long that I knew I would never be able to get to the end of it. I was loved. Always. Forever. No matter what.

Once again, joy erupted in my heart as I began to understand just a little bit more of the hugeness of the Lamb's love for me. I felt like leaping, dancing, twirling, shouting, laughing, and crying all at once.

Tears ran down my cheeks as I stood up, jumped across the distance that separated us and wrapped my arms around him in a giant lamb hug. "I love you!" I said. "Thank you for choosing to love me! Thank you for rescuing me! Thank you for setting me free! Thank you for giving me life."

I took a step back and then said, "And thank you for loving me. Always. Forever. No matter what."

13 - The Depths of Freedom

This is eternal life: that they know you, the only true God,
And Jesus Christ, whom you have sent.
(Book of Truth - John 17:3)

After this, the Lamb and I walked for some distance along the banks of the river. The day was warm, and the air was sweet. I cannot describe what it was like to walk and talk with the one who chose to delight in me, love me, and wholly accept me regardless of what I had done.

I thought I had known full freedom when the Lamb shattered my chains, setting me free from the sentence of death. But then, when I walked through the Narrow Gate and entered into the Kingdom of Light, I realized that the freedom the Lamb was giving me was not just freedom from death, but it included the liberty to live abundantly in his Kingdom of Light!

But now, as we spent time together, I understood more of the heart of the Lamb and his love for me. I realized that the freedom he was giving me was not just freedom from death and freedom to live, but also the freedom to be loved by him. Always. Forever. No matter what.

And with his love came the liberty to love him in return.

I honestly wondered if my mind would burst as its borders kept expanding with each new discovery of the Lamb. Imagine being told that since before the beginning of time, the Lamb had been waiting to spend time with you? Doesn't that rattle your mind a bit? It sure did mine. I still have trouble grasping it at times!

Not only had he been waiting since the beginning of time, but now that we were spending time together, he was showing me that our time spent together was the most important thing to him. I was his priority, and being together brought him great delight!

In those hours as we walked along the gurgling water, I began to understand that I was important and special to him. He, the Eternal One, the All-Knowing One, and the Almighty One had chosen to love me. Always. Forever. No matter what.

It was due to the completeness of his love for me that my heart was free to receive his love and to love him in return.

I wish I could share with you all that we talked about that day on our walk in the fresh grass along the banks of the river, but there were so many words spoken that it would take more time and space than I have in the pages of this journal.

But, there are two things I want to share with you. First, the Lamb showed me that because he had paid the debt of my sin and had chosen to love me – always, forever, no matter what – I would forever be accepted by him. He would never cast me aside. I did not have to live in fear of his rejection.

This was another mind-boggling truth because it was so different from what I had known in the Kingdom of Darkness. As a citizen there, I had been a chameleon, trying to balance the different expectations and demands of the people around me so that I would be accepted and not excluded. Yet, without fail, I found myself rejected again and again because I was never rich enough, pretty enough, funny enough, athletic enough, good enough…I am sure you get the picture.

At first, this truth of living as one loved and accepted, without fear of rejection, was hard to grasp. Thankfully, the Lamb is a patient teacher, and the longer I walked with him, the more he showed me that his love and acceptance for me was just as he had said.

He loved and accepted me. Always. Forever. No matter what.

The second thing that I want to share with you concerns the three gifts that the Lamb gave to me that day.

They were the most intriguing –

The most confusing –

The most puzzling –

Yet, the most needed gifts I have ever received!

14 - The First Gift

I have hidden your word in my heart that I might not sin against you.
Your word is a lamp for my feet, a light on my path.
(Book of Truth - Psalm 119:11, 105)

After we had been walking for some time, we drew near a group of trees so tightly woven together I could not see past their exterior. The Lamb walked straight towards the forest and stopped. The silver leaves which clothed the graceful arms of those trees filled the air with a happy tune of praise as the wind rustled past.

I watched in stunned amazement as the tribute of praise came to a close, and the trees bowed before the Lamb making an archway. He walked through the gap, and then looked back and called to me "Come!"

That was all the invitation I needed. My steps were quick as I stepped through the archway and into an inner room hidden within the grove. The moment I was through the doorway, the trees closed the opening and returned to their original positions.

The room I was in was circular with light grey walls made of the trunks of the trees. Above me, the branches of the trees were interlaced and intertwined in such a way that no part of the outside world could be seen. Light radiated from the silver leaves, filling the room in a sparkly glow. The grass carpeting the ground was so green and alive that my feet tingled as I walked to where the Lamb stood in the center of the room.

"What is this place?" I asked.

"This is the Gift Room," the Lamb said as he placed a small object in my hands. "This is my first gift for you."

In my hands was a leather-bound book. It was slightly longer and wider than my hand, and about one inch thick. A soft, golden glow shone from the book as I proceeded to open it. Its golden pages were filled with written words that pulsated with energy. The words seemed to be alive. The glimmer from the book bathed my feet in a light that pointed me in the direction of the Lamb. On the cover of the book was a title etched in golden lettering *"Book of Truth."*

"This Book of Truth is a record of my words," said the Lamb. "In its pages, you will find instructions that will teach and guide you on your journey through the Kingdom of Light. You will discover all my promises to you and the truth of who I am. You will find real-life accounts of others who have traveled this path that you are now on. Their stories are true. They are not made up, and they are included in this book to instruct you and to give you real examples of how they obeyed and put my words of truth into practice and what resulted when they did."

Here the Lamb paused for a moment. Sadness filled his eyes as he continued, "And what happened when they disobeyed and did not put my words of truth into practice."

The Lamb looked at me, and the intensity of his gaze captured mine like a magnet. I do not think I will ever forget the words that he spoke to me next. They were imprinted into my mind as surely as his words were written within the book.

"These words are not empty, useless words and there are no lies contained in the pages of this Book of Truth. These are my words of truth and love to you. They are your very life. Read them. Delight in them. Think about them. Believe them. Follow them. Do not turn from these words to the right or to the left. If you do these things I have told you, then it will go well for you in the Kingdom of Light." The Lamb gestured to the canopy of trees that surrounded us. "You will be like these trees that have been planted by a stream of water. Your leaves will not wither and dry up. You will bear fruit and whatever you do will prosper."

Here, my friend, I must pause in this story to tell you that on that day that I received the Book of Truth that contains the Lamb's words of instruction and promise, I did not fully understand what he meant, and I am still learning. But I can tell you, that the words in this Book are living and active. These words are a light to my feet that the Lamb has used to point me in the direction that I need to go or that I need to avoid. By these words, I have been warned, and in keeping them, there is a great reward. In not following them – well, let's just say that those are the places where trouble finds me. You will see examples of both in the pages that follow.

Now, back to the story.

After the Lamb finished giving me the Book of Truth, he placed another gift in my hand, and said, "This backpack works together with the Book of Truth. In it, you will find all the resources that you need as you journey through the Kingdom of Light."

Curious, I took the leather backpack and opened it. As I peered inside, I was surprised to discover that it was –

Completely empty.

15 - The Second Gift

And my God will meet all your needs
According to the riches of his glory in Christ Jesus.
(Book of Truth - Philippians 4:19)

To make sure that I was not missing something I should be seeing, I turned the backpack upside down and shook it. Nothing fell out. My first impression had been correct. The backpack was empty.

I turned the backpack the right way up again. I wasn't sure what to say. The Lamb had stated that it contained all the resources I needed for my journey. Was this a joke? If so, I did not understand its meaning. All I felt at that moment was a lot of confusion. I voiced my puzzlement to the Lamb. "Um, there is nothing in it."

The Lamb nodded and then instructed me to place the Book of Truth inside the backpack. It fit perfectly, but I was still bewildered. It almost seemed as if the Lamb was showing me that all I would need on my journey through the Kingdom of Light was this little book filled with his words of promise and instruction.

The Lamb took the backpack from my hands. "Remember I told you that my Book of Truth and this backpack work together? I had you place the Book of Truth into the backpack so that you would understand that anything you need is within the pages of this book. My promises will explain how I will provide for you. My instructions will show you the paths to walk on and the paths to avoid."

I nodded slowly. The pieces of the puzzle were beginning to come together in a way that I understood. "And you said that there are stories in this book about other people who have traveled through the Kingdom of Light. If I read their accounts, I can see how they trusted in your promises as they obeyed your instructions or how they disbelieved your promises as they disobeyed your instructions."

The Lamb nodded. "You are correct, but remember that you have to read this book to discover the promises, to learn the instructions and to find out how others who went before you lived. I have given this Book of Truth to many like yourself, but instead of reading it, they tuck it away and try to make the journey without knowing all that I have promised to give them."

He continued. "On your journey through the Kingdom of Light, I will supply for every need that you have, but only when you have that need. That is why the backpack is empty right now except for the Book of Truth. If I gave you right now all the resources that you needed for your journey, they would not even fit in this room. My provision for your need will always come. It will never be too early or too late. It will come just in time."

I stood there, holding the Book of Truth in my hands as I mentally put the pieces together in my mind of what he had told me. "So, all the instructions, promises, and provisions that I need to know for my journey through the Kingdom of Light I will find in this Book of Truth, and when I have a specific need that requires a specific resource I can look in the backpack and find it."

The Lamb smiled in agreement as he handed me the empty backpack. "You are beginning to understand how my Book of Truth and this Backpack of Provision work together. As you put what you are learning into practice, you will be able to understand these truths more clearly."

As soon as I took the backpack, it increased in size as it went from empty to full and became so heavy I nearly dropped it.

I placed it, along with the Book of Truth, on the ground. I opened the Backpack of Provision and looked inside. Surprised, I looked up at the Lamb. "Is this for me?"

The Lamb nodded. The joyful smile that had been on his face until this point was replaced with a solemn expression as he said, "This is the third gift that you will need for your journey through the Kingdom of Light."

Puzzled, I glanced back at the gift that was in my backpack. It was full of armor for a warrior. And the Lamb had said it was —

For me!

16 - The Third Gift

Put on the full armor of God,
So that you can take your stand against the devil's schemes.
(Book of Truth - Ephesians 6:11)

I reached inside the Backpack of Provision and pulled out a gleaming, silver sword that flashed with pure light. The grip of the handle was a perfect fit for my hand. It was light to carry, and it did not tire out my arm as I slashed it back and forth in the air. After a few more thrusts and jabs, I laid it on the ground and reached inside the backpack.

Next, I pulled out a shield that was taller than it was wide. When I placed the short edge on the ground and crouched down, I could entirely conceal myself behind it. Emblazoned on it were five letters that spelled the word "FAITH."

I laid the shield on the ground next to the sword. This time as I reached into the backpack, my hand snagged an object that puzzled me when I saw it. Its structure was like that of a helmet, clearly designed to protect the head. But, the addition of emeralds, rubies, diamonds, and sapphires made the helmet radiate with rainbow light, like the crown of royalty. It was beautiful, but what was it? A warrior's helmet or a warrior's crown?

After this, I pulled out a pair of leather boots, lightweight yet durable. A multitude of tiny nails covered the soles of those boots. They appeared to have the capability to dig into any surface and keep whoever was wearing them from slipping. I placed them on the ground next to the helmet and reached inside the backpack for the last two items.

I drew out a chainmail breastplate made of silver so pure it shone with white light, and the last item was a simple leather belt engraved with five letters that spelled the word "TRUTH." I set them down and took one last look inside the backpack.

Once again, it was empty. I set the backpack aside and then asked the Lamb again, "Are you sure these are for me?"

He nodded.

"Does this mean that I am a warrior?"

Again, he nodded.

"Don't I have to sign up to be in the army or go to school for military training? I have never been a soldier before."

This time the Lamb shook his head. "The moment that I broke your chains and set you free from the Kingdom of Darkness, you became a citizen of the Kingdom of Light, and my enemy became your enemy. My battle became your battle."

A shiver of panic slid down my spine. "Who is your enemy? What is your battle?"

"My enemy is the Prince of Darkness and his evil Hordes. My battle is the struggle between the light of truth and good against the darkness of lies and evil."

At that moment, I am not afraid to admit that my heart began to pound – hard! My hands began to sweat – a lot! As a former citizen of the Kingdom of Darkness, I knew well the power and the strength of the

Prince of Darkness and his Hordes. No one could stand in their way and overpower them.

No one except for the Lamb.

Reminded of this truth, a calm peace settled over my mind and my heart. Gone was the fear that had threatened to grab hold. I realized that this peace was one of the provisions that the Lamb had promised to provide just when I needed it. Because he knew me thoroughly, he knew what I needed when I needed it.

I took a deep breath and stated, "So, I am your warrior."

The Lamb affirmed my statement. "As my warrior, you do not fight this battle alone. You stand in my strength, the power by which I defeated the Prince of Darkness and his Hordes. Because the war is already won, you can stand firm in the position of victory."

I was confused. "If you won the war against the Prince of Darkness, why are there still battles to fight?"

"The Prince of Darkness hates me with a revulsion so venomous that he will stop at nothing to try and keep as many of people whom I created from entering the Kingdom of Light. Amongst those who become citizens of the Kingdom of Light, he prowls around like a roaring lion seeking whom he can tempt, deceive, and destroy."

The Lamb directed my attention to the armor. "With my strength and with this armor forged in my death and resurrection, you will be able to stand firm against his wicked schemes and the skirmishes he mounts to cause you to stray from the path that I have set before you."

He picked up the Belt of Truth and handed it to me. "Buckle this Belt of Truth around your waist. It will be the foundation that holds your armor together. This belt is constructed in my truth that is firm and steadfast. Because I do not change, it will not change. Ever. It is unshakeable in spite of the twisted lies that the Prince of Darkness speaks to try to deceive. His language is not the truth, for one of his nicknames is the Father of Lies. He can weave lies that sound so enticing they will tickle your ears with their sweet sounding words, yet they are so poisonous they can lead you astray. Your armor must begin with the Belt of Truth. It must be the standard by which you assess and determine the truthfulness of what you hear so that you will not be deceived and tripped up by the lies of the Evil Prince."

I took the belt and buckled it firmly about my waist.

Next, the Lamb handed me the breastplate. "This is the Breastplate of my Righteousness, and it is designed to protect your heart and your emotions. When the Prince wages his wicked schemes to cause you to doubt that you are saved or to feel guilty over sin that is forgiven or to condemn yourself for the debt of sin that I already paid for, this breastplate will protect your heart and your emotions. This is the Breastplate of my Righteousness, and I give it to you. Put it on and in doing so remember that you are redeemed, not because of the things that you have done, but because I paid the price for your sins. I defeated death. I conquered the grave. You are my child. You are a citizen of the Kingdom of Light and loved by me. You stand firm in the spotless purity of my righteousness. Hold onto this truth and believe it as you follow me."

I slipped on the Breastplate of Righteousness. It fit me perfectly, and I was thankful that my heart would be protected.

After this, the Lamb handed me the boots. I put them on, and they were not too big nor were they too small. It was another perfect fit. They were cool to my feet and gripped the ground so tightly I knew that it would be difficult for me to slip and fall with these boots on.

"You are right," the Lamb said in agreement with my thoughts. "With your feet protected by these Boots of the Gospel of Peace – my perfect peace – you will be able to stand firm. You will not slip when the Prince tries to trip you up with his temptations, accusations, and lies. You will come to know that the peace I give you will hold fast and remain firm in spite of the outer circumstances that you will face."

Then the Lamb handed me the Shield of Faith. I strapped it to my arm as the Lamb described to me that faith in him and his promises would be able to deflect the fiery arrows dipped in poison that the Prince and his Hordes used to mount attacks on the citizens of the Kingdom of Light. By taking up the Shield of Faith and firmly believing in the Lamb and his promises while following his instructions, I would be able to extinguish or snuff out all the fiery darts of the Evil Prince sent my way.

The next item the Lamb handed to me was the object that I could not tell if it was a helmet or a crown. I slipped it on, and again it fit perfectly. It was not heavy.

"This is the Helmet of Salvation," the Lamb said. "Use this to protect your mind against the lies that the Evil One will speak to cause you to doubt the truth of my promises and my instructions to you and the truth of your identity in me. The jewels on this helmet are to remind you of the truth of who you are and the truth of my promises to you."

"You are my child. I love you always. Forever. No matter what. My promises to you are sure and steadfast. I will be faithful to fulfill every single one. You must guard your mind with the truths that are yours because of your salvation. The Helmet of Salvation will garrison your mind so that the Evil Prince, also known as Satan and the Devil, will not be able to set up a stronghold of untruth in your mind."

Finally, the Lamb picked up the gleaming sword. He placed it into my hands. "This is the Sword of the Spirit, which is my word. When confronted with the lies, the deceit, and the temptations of the Evil Prince, you must use your sword accurately and precisely. For every lie that he will use to try to deceive you, there will be a specific word from the Book of Truth that you can thrust back at him. Do not try to argue or debate with him. You will lose. The only words that have any power against the strength of his lies are my words of truth because they are the words of life and light. To use this sword, take a firm hold of my words of truth and plunge them forward into the lies that are spoken."

That day, as I stood in the strength of the Lamb and clothed with his armor, I realized that my journey in this Kingdom of Light was going to be unlike anything I had ever known. Not only had I been saved, redeemed and delivered. Not only did I have full access to all the promises of the Lamb's Book of Truth and full rights as a citizen of the Kingdom of Light. Not only was I known fully by the Lamb. Not only was I loved and accepted by him unconditionally, without stipulations or prerequisites.

I was also a warrior who could stand firm against the schemes of the Prince of Darkness. Although I knew I did not have to live in fear of him, because he was already a defeated foe, I felt a little bit anxious and afraid.

And that was my first mistake, but I did not realize it until sometime later.

17 - The Door

…Knock and the door will be opened to you.
(Book of Truth - Matthew 7:7)

After I had my armor on, I placed the Book of Truth into the Backpack of Provision which had shrunk back to its standard size. I strapped it to the Belt of Truth and watched the Lamb walk to the wall of interlocking trees. He motioned for me to join him.

"It is time to leave this place and begin your journey in the Kingdom of Light. Remember that my words will be a lamp to your feet and a light to your path. Remember that I will provide for every need that you have when you need it. Remember that in my strength and with the armor I have given you, you can stand firm against the schemes of the Prince of Darkness."

I took a deep breath and nodded. I was resolved and ready to head out, but as I looked around the maze of trees that made up the walls of the Gift Room, I realized I had a problem. There was no door. How was I going to get out?

The Lamb had made the opening before, but now he just stood there watching me with a very amused expression in his eyes. I stared back at him for a moment and then began to move around the circle, trying to find a door so that I could get out. I walked around the circumference of the room, but my search only confirmed what I had thought.

I stood there silently for a moment, and finally stated the obvious, "There is no door."

The Lamb agreed. "You are right. There isn't."

"How can I get out?"

"Through the door, of course!" the Lamb laughed.

"But you just said that there was no door," I exclaimed, confused and frustrated. How was I supposed to go through a door that did not exist?

"Did I tell you that it is time to leave this place?" the Lamb questioned.

"Um, yes," I responded hesitantly.

The Lamb continued his quiz. "Will I always provide for everything that you need when you need it?"

"Yes, that is what you promised," I answered. "And you said that every promise you have made you will be forever faithful to fulfill."

"That is correct," said the Lamb. "You can know for certain that anything I ask you to do, I will provide what you need to do it. But before some promises are fulfilled, a step of obedience must be taken." He regarded me with serious eyes. "What do you need right now?"

"A door?"

"Again, you are right! But do you have one?"

"Obviously, no!" I responded with irritation – more at myself than the Lamb. I knew I must be forgetting something that I should remember.

He responded to my impatience with patience. "Where do you need to look for my instructions, promises, and provisions for you?"

Where was I supposed to look? Frustration in my mind began to mount but then evaporated as I remembered the instructions of the Lamb were in the Book of Truth. I reached into the backpack and pulled out the book. Somewhere in these pages would be instructions to direct me on how to find a door to get out of the grove of trees.

The Lamb looked over my shoulder and directed me to a part of the Book of Truth called "Matthew." From there, he took me to the seventh chapter, and then a smaller segment that also had the number 7. He said, "To help you find the promises and instructions easier, the Book of Truth is divided into many parts. The larger sections are books, and each has its own title. Within each book are smaller sections called chapters, and within each chapter are small segments called verses. The verse you just looked up is Matthew 7:7. This means this promise is in the book of Matthew, chapter 7, verse 7."

I vaguely remember bobbing my head up and down in acknowledgment to the Lamb, because the golden words that I was reading captivated my attention – *"Ask and it will be given to you; seek and you will find; knock and the door will be opened to you."*

I glanced at the trees and then the Lamb. Was it that simple?

The Lamb nodded, so I raised my hand and knocked on one of the trunks of the intertwined trees that stood in front of me. The silver leaves quivered as the branches shivered and a door appeared before me. I took one step forward and then another as I strode out into the sunlight.

18 - My First Battle

The weapons we fight with are not the weapons of the world.
On the contrary, they have divine power to demolish strongholds.
We demolish arguments and every pretension that sets itself up against
the knowledge of God, and we take captive every thought to make it
obedient to Christ.
(Book of Truth - 2. Corinthians 10: 4, 5)

One day spilled into the next day as the Lamb, and I walked through the green meadows and quiet waters of the Kingdom of Light. He spent much time teaching me his words of truth and showing me more of his promises and instructions contained in the Book of Truth that he had given me.

He showed me how to find the accounts of mighty heroes who combated whole armies, ferocious giants and hungry lions. As I read the recorded stories of these brave men and women, who took the steps of obedience ~~and went~~ to go wherever the Lamb sent them – even when it was hard and challenging – I was inspired. If the Lamb had helped them in their times of need ~~and if he had provided~~ providing all that they needed to do the work that he had given them to do, would he not do the same for me?

As we walked together through that country, there was a nagging question that tickled the back of my mind, and it would not go away. Each day it grew a bit by bit, and the larger it became, the harder it was to ignore. Finally, I could not overlook it any longer. How could this country be my home? *The question was this.*

You see, as I read through the Book of Truth, I realized that the citizens of the Kingdom were mighty heroes. In the book of Exodus, there was a guy named Moses whose parents courageously placed him in a basket made of grass and set their three-month-old baby adrift on the Nile River to keep him safe from the king of that land. When he grew up, Moses took on the role to rescue his people from the clutches of slavery that they suffered in that land.

There was another person named Joshua who battled nations and had such confident faith in God that when he needed more daylight to complete a battle, he asked God to make the sun stand still. And you know what? God did! Isn't that amazing?

I read about a girl in the book of Esther, who ~~even though she~~ *yet,* was a captive in a foreign land, she became the queen of the empire and then saved her people from annihilation.

But you know, as inspiring as these stories were to read, I felt the icy tentacles of fear and doubt begin to snake their way through the hallways of my mind. I had not sensed these feelings since I had entered the Kingdom of Light, but I recognized them well from my days spent in the Kingdom of Darkness. Together, fear and doubt created a confused chaos of disaster and disorder in my mind and heart. *If I was not a hero of courage —*

As I ~~doubted~~ *questioned* that the Kingdom of Light was my home, I wondered *As these doubts arrived* if my debt of sin had been fully paid. After all, the debt I owed had been huge! It was more than I could pay. How could the Lamb forgive a debt like that? Shouldn't I have to do something to earn his forgiveness and at least pay part of the debt?

61

From there, my thoughts ~~goes~~ *But that thought created another problem.*

But, if the Lamb didn't have the power to forgive all of my sins, how would he be able to provide for all of my needs? And if he couldn't meet all my needs, what would happen when I met the Prince of Darkness in battle? How would I be able to stand firm? As a former citizen of the Kingdom of Darkness, I had seen the strength of the power that the Prince of Darkness and his Hordes continually exercised.

As the threads of fear interlaced their way through my mind, I reached up to wipe the drips of sweat that were forming on my forehead. As I did so, my hand brushed against my Helmet of Salvation. As my fingers trailed over the jewels that were there, the truth of who the Lamb was and who I was because of him came flooding back to me.

I reached into my Backpack of Provision, pulled the Book of Truth and opened it to a promise that the Lamb had shown me in Colossians 1:13, 14 – *"For he has rescued us from the dominion of darkness and brought us into the kingdom of the Son he loves, in whom we have redemption, the forgiveness of sins."*

These words of truth began to combat the thoughts of fear and doubt that had been filling my mind. How could I have forgotten the moment the Lamb stepped onto the scales that held the weight of my sin and catapulted the debt of my sins so high and far away, not one speck remained. With that one act, my sins were forgiven, and I was rescued from the Kingdom of Darkness. The Lamb had broken my chains, set me free and brought me into his Kingdom of Light – my new home. In this place, I was loved and accepted. Always. Forever. No matter what.

As my mind continued to fill with these truths, the chains of fear and the threads of doubt that had been snaking through my thoughts fled. They could not stay in a place filled with the light of the Book of Truth.

Beside me, the Lamb smiled. "You are learning what it means to use the Helmet of Salvation. Well done!" Then his expression turned serious. "One of the favorite battlefields of the Evil Prince is in the mind.

It is in this battle that you must be diligent in taking captive every thought that you think."

"Take my thoughts captive?" I interrupted. "What does that mean?"

"How long have the questions and fear been lurking in your mind?" *The Lamb watched me intently & then asked,*

"Since I started reading about the heroes of faith in the Book of Truth."

"What about before that?" *the first fear had reflected back in time the first doubt that entered my mind*
I thought hard and realized that it had been while I was standing in the grove of trees receiving my gifts that I had had my original thought of fear at the prospect of meeting the Prince of Darkness in battle.

I looked at the Lamb, and he nodded his head. "That is right. One single thought of fear was the seed that took root. Those roots multiplied and grew. Soon, seeds of doubt were added, and as they rooted in your thoughts, you questioned if your debt was fully paid. If it wasn't, then that meant I had not been able to pay for it all. If I could not do that, how could I provide for every need and how could you stand firm against the Prince of Darkness?"

I shook my head. "All that started with just one seed of fear?"

The Lamb nodded. "That is one of the ways that the Prince of Darkness wages wars and sets up strongholds of untruth in your mind. He plants little seeds. If they take root, they quickly grow, affecting your thoughts and attitudes. Soon, their poison multiplies into doubting the truth of my promises and instructions to you. If the poison is allowed to spread further, it can seep into the actions that you take."

"The secret to demolishing the strongholds of untruth is to take every single thought captive. Rope it in and compare it with my words of truth. If there is a contradiction or if it doesn't agree, get rid of that thought. Don't let it become a stronghold in your mind."

The Lamb turned his gaze to the east. My eyes followed, and in the distance, I saw a rainbow shimmering like an emerald in a crystal sky radiating with pure light. Separating that place from the Kingdom of Light was a golden wall. It spread across the horizon as far as I could see in both directions. Again, an intense longing filled my heart to be in that place.

When the Lamb looked back at me, he spoke with a gentle voice filled with mighty power. "And don't forget to look up! Remember that one day you will walk through the Gates of Life and enter into Heaven – the final home I have prepared for you. There you will live forever and ever. Also, remember that I am always with you. Armed with these truths and ~~your Helmet of Salvation~~ my strength, and your armor you will be able to resist the schemes of the Prince of Darkness."

19 - Irresistible Aroma

Jesus answered, "It is written: 'Man shall not live on bread alone,
But on every word that comes from the mouth of God.'"
(Book of Truth - Matthew 4:4)

In the days that followed, I put into practice taking every thought captive and making it obedient to the truth that is in the Lamb's Book of Truth.

In the beginning, this was no easy task. Do you know how many thoughts go through a brain every day? It is a lot. I don't even know if there is a number that big!

But here is an interesting detail to keep in mind. I remembered the Lamb's promise to provide for every need that I had, so I asked him for wisdom to help me sort my thoughts so that I could determine which to keep and which to give the boot. I did not want fear and doubt to have the opportunity to take root in my mind again. I wanted the seeds of the Lamb's truth to take root. It was a drawn-out process, but slowly my pattern of thinking was being transformed.

As a new citizen of the Kingdom of Light, part of the process of transforming my mind was to spend time each day reading the Book of

Truth. A thought that took root in my mind and heart was that if I wanted to know more about the Lamb, his promises and his truth, it would be helpful to spend regular time with him and his word each day.

So began my journey of reading a small part of the Book of Truth each day. If I had a question, I could ask the Lamb to help me understand what I needed to know. He promised that every time I asked him for wisdom, he would give it to me abundantly. With time, I exchanged my old thought patterns from the Kingdom of Darkness for the new thought patterns of the Kingdom of Light. My thinking was being transformed.

I seemed to be making good progress, until one morning when I awoke to the most delicious aroma filling the air. It was a bit tangy, but oh, it smelled so good! The nose hairs in my nostrils tingled with delight. I stood up, stretched and tried to figure out from which direction the scent was coming. I had a fleeting thought that I should spend some time with the Lamb in his word again, but that could wait.

This aroma was too tempting to resist!

I sniffed the air. Yes, it was coming from the south. The wind seemed to be directing that flavorful air right to me. Even my taste buds started to quiver!

"Where do you want to read today?" the Lamb asked with curious eyes.

I shook my head and turned. The Lamb stood behind me holding out the Book of Truth. He repeated his question. "Where do you want to read today?"

A breeze of the sweetly perfumed air brushed past my face as the Lamb held out his words. As the wind increased, the smell grew stronger, and I felt caught in the middle of some great tug-of-war. Finally, I stuttered a response.

"Um, let's wait with the spending time together today, ok? I have to see what is filling the air with such an incredible aroma." With that, I turned my back on the Lamb, on spending time with him, and on reading his word. The smell seemed to be calling my name. It couldn't wait. As I left the Lamb behind, my steps quickened until I was running across an open meadow peppered with rocks. Then, it happened!

Wham! My foot struck one of those rocks. My arms windmilled as I tried to stop my inevitable crash, but it did little good. My momentum propelled me through the air, and I hit the ground hard. I took a moment to recapture the breath knocked out of my lungs, and then I stood up and brushed the dirt off my knees.

Ouch! I rolled up my pant legs and had a look. Yup! Both knees were scraped, bleeding and very tender to the touch. I suspected the wounds would leave scars. I gently covered up my bruised kneecaps and stood straight. I felt like I had forgotten something important, but what was it?

Oh yeah, the Lamb had asked me a question, but before I had time to ponder that thought too deeply, I got another whiff of that fantastic fragrance. Once again I was off. This time a bit slower, but with more determination.

I rounded a clump of trees and there it was! Oh, it smelled so good. I couldn't resist it. I hobbled as quickly as I could and hurled myself straight into –

The Slop Pit!

20 - Return to the Slop Pits

If we confess our sins, he is faithful and just and will
Forgive us our sins and purify us from all unrighteousness.
(Book of Truth - 1. John 1:9)

Oh, how wonderful it was to be back in the very pit that I had spent so much time in! I flung myself into the rotting mass of decay, delighting in the smell and the experience of wild abandonment.

The slimy green covering of the pit coated my skin. Decomposing rot tangled in my hair. I scooped up a handful of the slop and brought it to my mouth, savoring every decomposed chunk. I dove under the surface, swimming in the muck, reveling in the feel of the fetid, rancid swill as it brushed past my skin.

My head came to the surface. I took a deep breath and looked up. There on the edge of the Slop Pit stood a few members of the Horde. Laughter erupted from their maggot-filled faces. Eyes full of darkness stared at me. One of the Horde brushed back matted hair as he spoke, "We knew that smell would be too good for you to resist! You wouldn't be able to stay away!"

I paused in my reveling as nausea began to fill my stomach. I looked across the pit to the other side. The Lamb watched me with eyes so sad I had to look away. What had I done?

Frantically, I made my way to the edge of the Slop Pit. With desperation, I grasped at the clumps of dead grass that surrounded the pit and tried to pull myself out. But, it was of no use. I was stuck. I could not get out.

I tried to get rid of the putrid, decaying mass of rot that was clinging to my hair and clothes. But, it was of no use. I could not make myself clean.

Finally, I looked into the eyes of the Lamb. I remembered that he had said that he would love me. Always. Forever. No matter what. Did he still love me ~~now?~~ even though I had turned my back neglected him for the slop pit,

I hesitated for a moment and then called, "Please, help me!"

He reached down and drew me out of the mire. He set my feet on firm ground. I fell to my knees and cried, "I am sorry! Please forgive me!"

In that instant, the tangy scent in the air that had drawn me astray left and the rotten gunk clinging to me was removed. The Lamb made me clean. I looked up at him and saw him smile. He forgave me, and the truth that I didn't have to be perfect to the loved by the Lamb buried itself a little bit deeper into my heart.

He loved me. Always. Forever. No matter what.

Even when I messed up.

21 - The Valley of Death

God is our refuge and strength, an ever-present help in trouble.
The name of the Lord is a fortified tower;
The righteous run to it and are safe.
(Book of Truth – Psalm 46:1 and Proverbs 18:10)

After my venture in the Slop Pit, the friendship between the Lamb and I strengthened. Gradually, he sent me out on missions for him throughout the Kingdom of Light. I remember one assignment in particular. I was to carry a dispatch to another traveler in the Kingdom of Light. The message was a reminder that the Lamb was our place of refuge, strength, and safety. We could run to him and find the help we needed in times of trouble.

By nightfall, I had not arrived at my destination, so I set up camp on the trail under a rock outcropping that would provide some shelter from wind and possible rain. I ate a light meal and settled down to have a rest. I started to drift off into dreamland when I abruptly ~~journeyed back to the land of full~~ alertness. Fingers of unease trailed down my spine, sparking shivers throughout my whole being. I sat up and listened. The darkness was quiet, but the silence screamed at me. Something was not right.

I looked up into the black sky. The moon remained hidden behind the clouds. Its light peaked through the fringes of the veil that covered the sky. The ghostly outlines did not calm the fear rising in my heart. Rather, they caused my anxiety to turn into dread.

Cautiously, I reached over and pulled my backpack towards me. Holding it in my left hand, I let my fingers be my eyes as I brushed them over the hard ground to make sure that nothing had fallen out. Satisfied my supplies were in my pack, I stood up. Pressing my back against the rock that was behind me, I tried to blend into the rock face as I scanned the area surrounding me.

Something sinister was out there. Its presence hushed the songs of the night creatures. The crickets muted their friendly chirps. The owls' hoots were silent. The coyotes ceased their yipping at the moon.

I shivered as the seconds ticked past. Even though the warmth of the day still permeated the air, the dread that filled the air chilled me. I glanced up at the canopy of rock that jutted over the place I had set up camp. The ledge that I had thought would provide shelter from rain no longer seemed to be a source of protection. A few grains of dirt fell silently to the ground in front of me.

Whatever had awoken me was on the ledge five feet above me. What could I do?

As my heart raced and screamed at me to run, my mind tried to recapture the lay of the land before me. I was still on the path the Lamb had set before me. It was a trail that was nothing more than a ledge carved on the near vertical wall of a canyon. A vertical drop was on my right hand, and a cliff face was on my left. Since there was no place of protection behind me, the only way open was forward.

But, I didn't know what was in front of me. All I recalled was that the trail continued straight ahead for about thirty feet before it curved to the left and disappeared. I did not know what was around the bend, but if the Lamb had set me on this path to deliver a message, he would help me carry it out –

Wouldn't he?

Deciding to trust him, I balanced on my right foot and lifted my left so that I could tighten the laces of my Boots of Peace. If I had to make a fast sprint to outrun whatever danger was on the ledge above me, tripping would not help. After checking both boots, I put my backpack over my shoulders and prepared to make a surprise dash in hopes of gaining extra ground.

As I took in silent breaths, filling my lungs with oxygen, I noticed a faint but sour, decaying aroma in the air. I shuddered for it was the odor that accompanied the lethal groups of dog-wolves that went ahead of the Horde armies, scouting for and sniffing out their prey. The packs were ruthless, deadly, and rarely ever alone. If there was one above me on the ledge, others would be hiding and waiting for the order to attack me.

I needed help. If the enemy was surrounding me – and I was convinced it was – a mad dash would only postpone the inevitable by a few seconds. I pulled out the Book of Truth, remembering that the Lamb had told me his words of truth were a lamp to my feet and a light to my path. Its light radiated in the darkness on the trail in front of me, and its pages opened to a part of the message he had given me to deliver – "*The name of the Lord is a fortified tower. The righteous run to it and are safe.*"

As I read these words, one word, in particular, caught my attention. Run.

The enemy above me growled menacingly. Another one answered not far behind me. It was time to move. I had to get out of there.

Gripping the book tightly, I breathed a silent cry for help and bolted from the small crevice. As I raced down the path, the light from the book shone out before me, guiding my feet. I heard a soft thud on the ground as the dog-wolf landed behind me. He howled savagely, and the baying of several others responded to his cry.

I leaned to left as I raced around the corner of the path. In front of me, a door stood wide open. I ran into it, and the door closed tight behind me – all on its own. I doubled over and took in great gulps of air to steady my breath. Outside the dog-wolves savagely growled as they tried to breach the stronghold I was in. They pawed at the door, but their attempts were useless. The door that opened to me was firmly shut to them.

My heart rate lessened, and I stood straighter to look around the structure I was in. The light from the book glowed in the darkness, and I saw that I was in a circular room. Along the rock wall was a staircase that spiraled upwards.

Curious, I ventured up the steps and found a trapdoor at the top. I pushed it open and stepped onto circular platform edged with a three foot high stone wall. I sat down and leaned against the smooth rocks. Somehow, I knew that here, in this place, I was safe. I drifted off into a peaceful sleep.

When I awoke, pink and orange painted the eastern sky. It would not be long until the sun greeted the morning. Curious as to where I was, I stood and looked over the edge. I was standing on a floor that was thirty feet above the ground. From this vantage point, I could see the path on which I had made my scared dash last night. It ended at the base of this building that was cut into the side of the canyon wall.

Taking a step back, I saw a gold plate fixed to the side of the wall with these words – *"The name of the Lord is a fortified tower; the righteous run to it and are safe."*

They were the same words that were in the message I was to deliver! They were the same words that I read in the Book of Truth just before I prayed for help and darted out from my temporary camp.

Could it be? I looked around and saw that I was in a tower that had kept me safe – just as the words in the book had promised. I descended the stairs and saw that the door which had closed so firmly the night before, now stood open. As I ventured onto the trail to continue my mission, I said a prayer of thanks to the Lamb. His name was a strong tower to which I ran and found safety. Not only would I be able to deliver the Lamb's message, but now I would have a story to share of how the Lamb had used this exact verse to keep me safe.

22 - The Mountain

"Truly I tell you, if you have faith as small as a mustard seed,
You can say to this mountain, 'Move from here to there,' and
It will move. Nothing will be impossible for you."
(Book of Truth - Matthew 17:20)

"You want me to go through that?" my voice squeaked with bewilderment. "That's impossible."

"Did I say you had to go through it?" the Lamb questioned.

"Well, no," I stuttered. "But there is no way around it!"

The Lamb looked at me. "Did I say I wanted you to go around it?"

"Well, no," I sputtered. "Surely you don't mean for me to dig under it?"

The Lamb chuckled. "Did I say that I wanted you to go under it?

"Well, no! But surely you don't want me to go over it?"

The Lamb looked at me with calm, amused eyes. "Did I tell you to go over it?"

Speechless, I shook my head. The Lamb had given me another mission to carry out, but the path he had set before me had a massive obstacle that prevented me from continuing my journey. The route was entirely blocked by a mountain so vast, so colossal, and so gigantic, there was no way through it, over it, under it, around it or over it.

"Are you sure this is where I am supposed to be?" I asked the Lamb.

He nodded.

"And there is a way to get past this mountain?"

Again, the Lamb nodded and then said, "Why don't you look in your backpack and see what I have provided for you to do this thing that you call impossible?"

My backpack! Can you believe it? I had been so busy trying to solve the impossible problem in front of me that I had forgotten to see what the Lamb had provided for me to use. Eagerly I dug in my backpack. Surely there would be some dynamite or TNT or maybe a small atomic bomb! However, all I found was a case about the size of my thumbnail. I pulled it out and opened the lid.

Can you guess what was in it?

A seed.

A seed so small, I could hardly see it! How was I going to move this monstrosity of a mountain with a seed the size of a pin? Instructions were attached to the seed's container – "*If you have faith as small as a mustard seed, you can say to this mountain, 'Move from here to there,' and it will move. Nothing will be impossible for you.*"

Quizzically, I looked at the seed and then at the Lamb. The faith of a mustard seed?

As the Lamb's eyes bored into mine, I knew the next question he asked would be an important one.

"Do you trust me?"

As those four words tumbled in my mind, I thought of all that the Lamb had done for me. He rescued me, gave me life, forgave me, loved me unconditionally, accepted me, protected me, and provided for every need. He had proven himself to be entirely trustworthy. How could I not trust him? *He didn't want me to trust my ability to accomplish what he asked. He wanted my faith to be firmly placed on him.*

So, I nodded my head and answered, "Yes." *Little faith in the Lamb. Little faith in the Lamb could accomplish far more than my trust in my strength.*

The Lamb smiled, and said, "Plant the seed."

I took that seed and found a small place on the ground where the dirt was soft. I made a small hole in the ground, placed the seed inside, watered it and patted dirt over the top.

Then, I sat down beside the Lamb and waited.

That seed must have had some superior, growing strength because within a few minutes a tender green shoot pushed its way out of the dirt. Its leaves opened as it reached upwards to the sunlight. Steadily it grew in size and strength.

"The sun is giving the plant the nutrients that it needs to grow," *explained* the Lamb. "And even though it is hidden from the eye, its roots are pushing down deep into the heart of the mountain."

I felt a small tremor quiver the ground under my feet, and then a tiny crevice appeared between the plant and the mound of rock. It fractured into many channels, each one snaking its way across the ground to various points along the base of the mountain.

Another tremor shook the ground, but the plant did not quiver. It stood firm and fast, while the mountain trembled and shuddered. Small pebbles spilled down its sides. Soon those pebbles were chased by granite boulders. For one moment the mountain stood tall and commanding, silhouetted against the sky, and then with one mighty heave, the ground opened wide its mouth, and the mountain disappeared as it fell into the heart of the earth.

As the dust settled, I jumped up and ran to the spot where the mountain had once stood, *and* peered at the ground. Not one trace of the mountain was left. In its place, I found the path that the Lamb had set before me to take.

The Lamb came and stood beside me. "When you are walking on the path that I have set before you, carrying out the work I have given you to do, and you find the way blocked by a mountain that is impossible to move, remember this truth. Small faith firmly set on me is a faith that can ~~can do a~~ accomplishes far more move mountains." than great trust in your strength

Awe and wonder filled my heart as I walked in step with the Lamb on that path where the mountain had once blocked my way. Silently, I pondered the lesson that I had just learned. A little faith in the Lamb will do much more than

By faith in the Lamb, the mountain had moved! huge faith in

By faith in the Lamb, the impossible became possible! my ~~ability to~~ my strength

23 - Mission into the Kingdom of Darkness

"Therefore go and make disciples of all nations…"
(Book of Truth - Matthew 28:19)

Another mission the Lamb sent me on took me deep into the heart of the Kingdom of Darkness. I was to bring news of the light of the Lamb to a slave named Tillie who was in the clutches of the Prince of Darkness. This mission was urgent, for the Lamb had revealed to me that she would soon be brought to the Slave Market. If she did not know the good news that by putting her trust in the Lamb, he would pay her debt of sin and free her from her chains, she would face the Gates of Death without hope.

As I moved forward on the path before me, my attention was focused on the dreary horizon. There I saw groves of trees – grey and lifeless – lifting skeletal arms upward to the gloomy sky. Wisps of smoke crawled along the ground as the pungent odor of decay and rot filled the air. Black birds – the Scavengers of Death – swirled in the air, cawing and squawking, as their ravenous gaze swept over the ground in search for more food.

Whisper soft, I felt a bug creep up my arm and my neck. In two swipes I sent them flying to the ground. Or so I thought. I glanced down but did not see them. I felt others crawling on my leg, arm, neck, and spine. It reminded me of the maggots that used to feed on my flesh when I had been a citizen of the Kingdom of Darkness. Frantically, I reached my right hand across to swipe the ~~insects~~ larvae away, but when I glanced at my left arm, there was nothing there. My skin was as clear as it had been since the day the Lamb redeemed me.

I swiped my shoulder and scratched my leg. What was happening? My flesh felt like it was covered in millions of the squiggling, white larvae, burrowing deeper into my skin with each painful bite that they took. Yet, when I looked at my skin, nothing was there.

But the sensations that I felt were so real!

I ripped off my Helmet of Salvation, letting it drop to the ground as I scratched my head vigorously. Every strand of my hair felt like it had been transformed into those insects of decay that loved to feed on the flesh of the citizens of the Kingdom of Darkness.

What did this all mean? How could I be a citizen of the Kingdom of Light and feel these pests? Was it possible that the Lamb's power was not strong enough to protect me from the devices of the Prince of Darkness?

As I continued to rub my head, doubts began to fill my mind. Maybe I wasn't a citizen of the Kingdom of Light. Maybe my rescue was an allusion. As doubts continued, fear gripped me. How could I go on a mission for the Lamb if he couldn't protect me? As these thoughts swirled within me, my gaze fell on the Helmet of Salvation that lay on the ground by my feet. One of the rubies refracted and twinkled in the rays of the moonlight, and I remembered what the Lamb had told me when he placed the Helmet of Salvation on my head.

"Use this helmet to protect your mind against the lies that the Evil One will speak to cause you to doubt the truth of my promises to you and the truth of your identity in me. The jewels on this helmet are to remind you of the truth of who you are and the truth of my promises to you."

I picked up the Helmet of Salvation, placed it on my head and reached into my backpack to pull out the Book of Truth. I turned to Colossians 1:12, 13 – *"And giving joyful thanks to the Father, who has qualified you to share in the inheritance of his holy people in the kingdom of light. For he has rescued us from the dominion of darkness and brought us into the kingdom of the Son he loves."*

As this light of truth radiated through my mind the torment caused by the sensations of the maggots fled. The trickery of the Prince of Darkness was not powerful enough to overpower and overcome the truth that by his death and resurrection, the Lamb had ~~truly~~ entirely rescued me from the Kingdom of Darkness and completely made me a citizen of the Kingdom of Light.

Before continuing on my journey, I knelt and thanked the Lamb for rescuing me from the trickery of the Prince of Darkness. Even though the sensations of the maggots seemed genuine, they were not a reality. The truth was that I had been rescued from the Kingdom of Darkness and brought into the Kingdom of Light. What I once had been, I no longer was.

I continued on my mission into the Kingdom of Darkness and reflected on the fact that this incident was a good reminder that I needed to be on my guard against the traps and illusions put on my path by the Prince of Darkness.

He did not want me to move forward on this mission.

24 - Before the Beginning of Time

…you were redeemed…
With the precious blood of Christ, a lamb without blemish or defect.
He was chosen before the creation of the world…
(Book of Truth - 1. Peter 1:18 – 20)

As dawn began to break over the horizon, I stopped to rest. After eating some food and having a small drink, I pulled out a booklet that I had received from another citizen of the Kingdom of Light describing lessons learned from the Book of Truth while following the Lamb. Its title was "Before the Beginning of Time." Curious, I opened the pages and began to read.

In the realm of eternity, before time began, the Great King who is sovereign over all that has been, that is, and that ever will be –

Had a plan.

It was a brave plan. An intricate plan. A costly plan.

It was a plan whose scope was so huge, enormous and vast that it spanned from the realm of his throne in eternity to the universe full of life that he would speak into existence by the very power of his words.

It was a plan rooted in the depths of his heart of love and his desire to know, delight in, and talk with the most precious, yet marvelous wonder that he would fashion in his image with his own hands. Into this creation, he would breathe the breath of life, and his creation would become a living being.

Human.

And so at a time divinely chosen, a word was spoken, and light burst forth as the clock of time began. The Great King was enacting his plan to create for himself a universe. A world. A people.

When everything was done, the Great King – the Creator of Life – exclaimed, "It is very good!"

And indeed, it was good. No death, disease, or pain existed in this new world. There was only light, goodness and life as the sounds of creation filled the air. Water gurgled within its banks as leaves danced softly in the fingers of a gentle wind. Birds sang songs of praise given them by their Creator as they fluttered and flew with their multi-colored wings. Vivid water creatures of all sizes leaped out of the water before plunging back into the depths of the home fashioned for them. On land, the sounds of the multitudes of animals created a beautiful symphony. Every part of the Great King's creation delighted in the gift of life that had been given to them by their Creator.

Now out of the dust on the earth, the Great King had fashioned with his own hands his most crowning achievement. Man. Woman.

He created them as a reflection of himself. No, they were not little gods. They were a people, made in his image, gifted with talents and skills so they could design, reason and look after their home – the world and the life that was contained within it.

Woven within their very design, the Great King also placed the ability to communicate so that they could understand and converse with him. His intention was not to separate himself from his creation but to be present within the lives of these, his people, whom he loved and with whom he delighted to know and converse.

But, as light and life filled the earth, a mighty battle took place in the heavenly realms, the home of the Great King. For within the heart of one of the Great King's servants named Lucifer – the most beautiful of all his angels – a rebellious plan was taking root. It was a plot so sinister and dark in its being that it overcame the light of truth that had once filled the heart of this now Evil Prince.

His choice was a simple one for he desired to take over the throne of the Great King – God Almighty – who was sovereign overall.

But, this truth did not deter the Evil Prince. He plotted, schemed, and strategized to make himself like the Most High and sit as high king over all. Many other angels joined in this evil plot of rebellion and revolted against the Great King. It was a clash between darkness and light. Holiness and wickedness. Truth and lies.

The Great King prevailed, and the Evil Prince was cast down out of the courts of heaven. His new home would be a place known as the Kingdom of Darkness. Here he would reign as until time had run its course. In the darkness of that kingdom, the Prince of Darkness and his evil Hordes – those angels who had joined him in his rebellion – delighted in thoughts so dark, so evil, and so sinisterly wicked in their design that their end – and who chose to take part in them – would be destruction.

The Evil Prince searched for ways to extend the borders of his Kingdom of Darkness. Lurking in the shadows of the earth, he observed the Great King's delight in and love for the life he had created. As the Prince of Darkness continued to watch, a sinister plan took shape in his evil mind. He noticed that the people with whom the Great King communicated with each day had been granted, by their Creator, a free will that gave them the ability to make decisions and choices.

His plan was a simple one. What if the truth spoken and the instructions given by the Great King were deceptively twisted so that the choice taken brought rebellion against the Great King? Would not this creation, so precious and beloved in the sight and heart of the Great King, then be cast out from of his presence just as he, the Prince of Darkness, had been?

A foreboding gleam, fueled by pure evil, began to glow in his eyes, for he knew that should the people turn against the Great King, the plan of the Almighty God would be foiled, thwarted, and halted.

Instead of life, death would reign.

Instead of light, darkness.

Instead of peace, rebellion.

Instead of truth, lies.

The Prince of Darkness disguised himself and went to the people. With cleverly cloaked words sweetened with the poison of lies, he tempted them with a choice to rebel against the words of the Great King.

For one moment, silence hung in the air, and then with the sound of one sweet bite, the most wicked, sinister laugh of all time erupted from the throat of the Prince of Darkness. He had succeeded!

The light was shattered, and now darkness would be supreme in this kingdom where he would reign. Death and separation from the Great King would be the penalty for all who ever lived, for the seed of sin would be passed on to each human descendant. In their hearts, each one would rebel against the Great King and fall short of his glory.

The Prince of Darkness lifted himself high – nothing could stop him now!

Except –

Except for a mystery that the Prince did not know. A mystery known only to the Great King. A mystery that would be revealed at just the right time.

For, you see, the Great King, had a sovereign plan to redeem his creation with a light –

A light powerful enough to shatter the darkness.

Who is this light?

He is the Lamb.

Slowly I closed the covers of the booklet and returned it to my backpack, reflecting on what I had just read. The Lamb had been sent on a mission by the Great King to be the light that would shatter the darkness that reigned in the Kingdom of Darkness. I took courage from his example, for I was walking in footsteps he had already walked. I was bringing the light of his truth to a slave named Tillie who was bound to the Evil Prince. If she accepted and believed this truth, once again, the light of the Lamb would –

Shatter the darkness.

25 -The Roaring Lion

Be alert and of sober mind. Your enemy the devil prowls around like a roaring lion looking for someone to devour. Resist him, standing firm in the faith…Finally, be strong in the Lord and in his mighty power.
(Book of Truth – 1. Peter 5:8 and Ephesians 6: 10)

Refreshed from a small rest, I pressed onward to complete the mission the Lamb had assigned to me. A north wind chilled the air as day turned into night, and I firmly placed one foot in front of the other.

Above me, the silent voices of the moon and stars rang out proclaiming the glory of the one who had created them. They twinkled at me with a soft light, reminding me to look up to remember an important truth. The one who knew each one of their names and held them in place was the same one who knew my name and held me in place. He was the Lamb, and he was the one who directed my steps on this path that led me to a stronghold of the Kingdom of Darkness.

As reassuring as that truth was, I could not stop the tremor that shivered through my body as I looked at the darkness that filled the horizon in front of me. It pulsed with a blackness so powerful that it made the moonlight around me seem like day. From the blackest part of the darkness, shadowy wisps trailed along the ground towards me. Already some of them were clawing at my feet, obscuring the path in front of me.

Honestly, this was not a path I would have chosen on my own. It was dangerous, scary, and unknown to me. Following the paths the Lamb set before me required greater trust in him and his truth than in what I could physically see. He told me this was learning to walk by faith – trusting that his presence, provisions, and promises were more real than what I could see around me. It was by faith in him, that the impossible became possible, much like the gigantic mountain had been removed by a small seed.

As I pushed onward, the light of the moon lessened, and the strength of the darkness increased. Yet, as I looked up, through the tendrils of dark murkiness, I could see ribbons of starlight shining above the blackness. In the same way, even though the Prince of Darkness was powerful and his kingdom was formidable, the Great King was Almighty – there was none stronger. His sovereign plan to shatter the darkness with the light of the Lamb was still being accomplished in the hearts of those who were held prisoner by the Prince of Darkness. The chains that bound them were shattered when they chose to believe in the good news of the Lamb.

In the dim light of the moon, I saw that my path was taking me straight into a grove of gnarled trees whose leafless branches groaned sinisterly in the wind. The chill of the night sank deeper into my being as I approached the entrance crisscrossed with shadows that gave the allusion of filling the ground with jagged spikes. As I entered that spooky copse of lifeless trees, and my senses screamed at me to turn around and find another way. But, this was the path that the Lamb had put me on. I needed to trust him and stay on it even if the way left my heart thumping in fear.

Continuing forward, I reached for the Book of Truth. Its pages opened to Joshua 1:9 – *"Have I not commanded you? Be strong and courageous.*

Do not be afraid; do not be discouraged, for the Lord your God will be with you wherever you go."

The Lamb often reminded me that he was always with me, even if I could not see him. Remembering this truth, courage took root in my heart for I knew that though the way ahead of me was dark and scary, I was not alone. I placed the Book of Truth back into my backpack and continued forward.

Moments later, a dark shadow slashed across the ground in front of me and then disappeared into a thicket of shrubs that bordered the path. My feet halted as my heart rate spiked. The movement had been so swift and silent, I wondered if it was my imagination. Yet, twenty feet ahead, alongside a dense thicket that bordered the path, was a rope snaking along the ground. The brush shivered with a slight movement, and the rope twitched to the right and to the left. The action reminded me of a cat's tail just before the cat pounced on its victim.

With a menacing roar designed to instill fear and dread into the hearts of its prey, a lion leaped onto the path in front of me. He crouched low to the ground and crept towards me. on feet with claws extended His eyes bore into mine, and I knew that he intended to devour me. Whole.

He emitted another roar that left the ground trembling beneath my feet, ~~and~~ I saw his fangs drip with rancid, acidic blackness that sizzled the ~~burned~~ the dirt with each drop.

While everything in me screamed to turn around and run away, I knew that I had to stand firm. I could not afford to give in to the fear and dread that was lurking at the corners of my mind. I had to stay alert and clear minded. I raised my Shield of Faith and the Sword of the Spirit while I stood my ground. Light flashed out of the end of my sword as words that I recently read from the Book of Truth came blazing to my mind – "*Be alert and sober minded. Your enemy the devil prowls around like a roaring lion looking for someone to devour. Resist him, standing firm in the faith…*"

As I stared at the advancing lion, the blackness of his eyes tried to pierce my soul with dread. The roar from his mouth was intended to send my feet running. When I didn't run, he drew himself up onto his hind legs. His size dwarfed anything around me, but I felt like a grasshopper in his presence. I knew that if I turned my back to escape, he would pounce and my journey would be over.

As I stood my ground and resisted him, light shot out of my sword again as another word of truth rippled through my mind with ringing clarity – "*Be strong in the Lord and in his mighty power.*"

To stand firm against my adversary I could not rely on my own determination. I had to find strength in the power of the Lamb.

The lion roared again, and I frantically whispered, "Help me to stand!"

When I didn't back down, the lion opened his wide mouth from the recesses of his throat, and flew at me, followed then another. Each one hit my Shield of Faith, shooting out sparks of orange and yellow before falling harmlessly to the ground.

Not one pierced me.

Dressed in the armor that the Lamb had given to me and relying on the strength of his power, I was able to stand my ground against the lion.

As the strength of the Lamb filled me, I raised my sword and pointed it at the lion. Light streaked through the darkness and hit the lion as I spoke these words of truth – "*Be strong and courageous. Do not be afraid; do not be discouraged, for the Lord your God will be with you wherever you go.*"

The lion backed away and then slinked into the dark shadows of the forest.

For several minutes, I did not move. I continued to stand my ground, holding the Shield of Faith in one hand and the Sword of the Spirit in the other. Specific sayings of the Lamb had not only given me the courage to stand firm and hold fast to my Shield of Faith, but those same words of truth had also activated my sword to shoot light into the darkness of the fear and dread that surrounded the lion.

Finally, with a firm grasp on my shield and sword, I moved forward slowly and steadily. Although I was relieved the lion did not return, and my body screamed for a rest, I knew that I could not stop here. I moved forward, eager to get out of those spooky woods. With each step I took, I could feel the eyes of the unseen enemies on me. Shivers traveled up and down my spine as I continued on the path. I needed to get out into the open.

I did not want to wait around and discover what might be hidden in the dark recesses of those trees.

26 - The Distraction of Deception

But each person is tempted when they are dragged away
By their own evil desire and enticed.
(Book of Truth - James 1:14)

As I left the dense grove of trees, I continued forward, putting some distance between me and that foreboding place. Finally, I found a spot on the path where I felt I could stop and rest.

The night had been long. After the encounter with the ~~lion~~ enemy, my senses and muscles had been on high alert, but thankfully I had not confronted the lion again. I sat down on the ground and drew my knees into my chest, trying to get warm. Even though a new day had dawned, a blanket of cold darkness continued to fill the air and block out the full light of the sun.

I took a deep breath and allowed my muscles to unwind as I scanned the environment around me. In front of me was a treeless plain, covered with depressing and colorless shades of grey. It stretched on until the sky and the ground merged into one. To my right, a few paces off the path, I noticed a small splash of red that contrasted vibrantly with the grey that seemed to coat every aspect of that land.

Curious, I got up and took a step towards the plant that dared to boldly grow in such a harsh environment. As I stepped closer, a sweet, fragrant aroma filled the air. I knelt to inspect the delicate, red blossoms and breathe in their rich scent. As I reached out my hand to pick one of them, pin pricks of pain shot into my fingers. I withdrew my hand and saw that several small thorns decorated my fingertips. As I struggled to remove the prickles, I contemplated these sweet-smelling, but painful-to-touch flowers, and my gaze wandered back to the path of the Lamb I had left behind. If I had not left the path, I would not have been pierced with the barbs.

I turned back to the path, but once again the air was filled with the sweet perfume. I closed my eyes as the fragrance filled my mind, and I felt an overwhelming desire to lay down my weapons. When I opened my eyes, I noticed an archway several feet in front of me. It was decorated with more of the delicate blossoms like the one beside me. The doorway led to a gazebo surrounded by a green pasture with a bubbling brook running through it.

The peacefulness of that place invited me to rest my weary body, mind, and soul in its tranquility. I could recuperate my strength before I continued on my mission for the Lamb. Surely, it wouldn't hurt to stop at this little out of the way place and have a small rest, even though it was not on the path. The Lamb would understand. As this thought grew increasingly welcome in my mind, my heart would not yield so easily for this pasture was not on the path the Lamb had set before me.

As I wavered, a soft wind blew past me. Its fingers brushed past my face, and I set down my sword and shield so I could remove my helmet, and let the breeze cool my head. I turned into the wind and walked towards the archway. The moment I stepped through it, chains snaked around my ankles and bound my wrists. The green pasture with the bubbling brook disappeared. I tried to get free and return to the path, but I was firmly bound by chains from which I could not get free.

Desperation filled me as I realized I was trapped. It had all been an illusion – a deception to ensnare me and keep me from moving forward on the path the Lamb had set before me. A path on which I had been free, even though it was painful and difficult at times.

As I struggled to break loose from the chains, I heard a malicious laugh beside me. Turning, I saw my enemy, the Prince of Darkness. He stood in front of me and said, "You resisted when I opposed you face to face, but when I offered you a chance to fulfill your need to rest in your own way, you forgot to resist. The fragrance of my deception was so sweet; your mind grabbed hold of it until you were nearly convinced that this was the right way - even though this was not on the path the Lamb set before you."

He drew closer until I could feel his hot breath on my face. The odor of decay was so overpowering my stomach recoiled. I tried to back up and to get away, but my chains held me fast.

He laughed and continued his rampage, "You forgot that I am your enemy, skilled in deception and intent on destruction. Your destruction. Yes, I am a roaring lion seeking to devour, but sometimes, when my ferocious roar is not enough to scare someone from the path of the Lamb, I will camouflage my trickery in a cloak of light and beauty. By enticing you and appealing to the fulfillment of your needs apart from the Lamb, I simply led you off his path and ensnared you."

With those words, the Prince of Darkness turned his back and left me. Chained. Alone. Helpless. Overhead I saw the Scavengers of Death begin to encircle the space above me. The sight of them spurred me on to try to get free. As I struggled, wounds around my wrists and ankles deepened as blood pulsed from them. They would leave scars, but as the screeches above me increased in their frenzy, I ignored the pain and continued to my struggle. Fear of what would happen if I did not get free fueled my efforts. In this wilderness, without any water, it would only be a matter of time before the scavengers descended and began to feed on my carcass.

After I expended my energy, shame and hopelessness filled my heart as I condemned myself for being such a fool. Wearily, I slumped to the ground and closed my eyes.

Who would save me now?

27 – To Return to the Path

He brought them out of darkness, the utter darkness,

And broke away their chains.

(Book of Truth - Psalm 107:14)

I heard the clink of a chain snapping and felt the release of the tightness that had surrounded my left wrist. I groaned in pain as the removal of the bands of metal reopened the wounds that had begun to scab. I opened my eyes and saw the Lamb next to me. I struggled to sit up as he released all the chains that bound me. Then, he placed in my hands a cup of water as he washed my wounds.

The sweet coolness of that living water revived my body and my soul, and I regained my strength to stand. However, before I stood, I knelt before the Lamb.

"I am sorry! How could have I been so stupid to leave the path that you set before me to walk on?" Shame filled my heart again, and I was sure that the Lamb would condemn me for my foolishness.

But I was wrong.

The Lamb raised me to my feet and said, "I forgive you, and I do not condemn you." He gazed at me with a steely glint in his eye as he said firmly, "Do not condemn yourself. My death and resurrection freed you from the penalty and condemnation of all your sin – past, present and future. You cannot be condemned again because I have paid the sentence of your sin."

I shook my head in disagreement, "But I went off your path, although I knew I should stay on it. I left my shield, sword, and helmet behind."

"Do you remember what happened when you went to the slop pits?" the Lamb questioned.

I nodded. How could I forget the time I ran full throttle into a slop pit of rotting, decaying matter? I still had scars on my knees from that day.

The Lamb's voice broke into my thoughts. "How did you get out?"

I shook my head. "I didn't. When I called for help, you were there to pull me out. When I said I was sorry; you forgave me and made me clean."

The Lamb nodded. "And whenever you fall into sin I will do that again and again and again. Sin doesn't change your position or who you are. Even when you sin, I still love you, and you will remain a citizen of the Kingdom of Light. Nothing can change that. The Prince of Darkness would love to keep you trapped in chains of shame and condemnation because then you will be hindered in completing the mission I have sent you on."

The mission! I had forgotten all about it. Was it too late to keep on going? Had I ruined everything?

As I watched the Lamb shake his head, I remembered he knew my thoughts.

"No, you did not ruin everything," he said as he returned my sword, shield, and helmet to me. "I am going to work this for your good.

Now you are wiser to the deceptions of the Prince of Darkness, and you will not stumble so easily next time." of Salvation

I placed my Helmet on my head, clipped my sword of the Spirit to my Belt of Truth, and clasped my Shield of Faith in my hand. "And now I understand that when I sin, I am not condemned again, because your death paid for every sin that I will ever commit – past, present, and future." I paused, and then asked, "Aren't you afraid that people who have chosen to follow you will take advantage of your forgiveness and just keep on sinning?"

As the Lamb and I returned to his path, he smiled sadly. "There will be those who think that my forgiveness provides them with the freedom to keep on living a life of sin. And there will be those who think that by putting their trust and efforts into following a list of rules, they have put safeguards in place to keep them from falling into sin."

"But both are distractions that keep them from realizing the full purpose of why I died for them. When people believe in me and accept my payment for their sins, their chains are broken. No longer is their destiny death for they receive eternal life. But, eternal life is more than just being saved from the Evil Prince and the Gates of Death. It is more than being able to live forever in heaven. Ultimately, eternal life is knowing the Great King, and myself, the Lamb who he sent into the world to shatter the darkness."

I nodded my head. I could understand what the Lamb was saying. At first, when he rescued me, I was thankful my destiny was no longer death and that I was free from the chains of sin. Then, as I stepped through the Narrow Gate and entered the Kingdom of Light, I was amazed and delighted in the abundance of the new life and living hope that he gave me. But, as we walked together, that I discovered he loved me always, forever, no matter what. Not only that, he delighted in me and accepted me.

It was as I came to know the Lamb, that these truths that captured my heart. As they took root in my life, I found that I loved the Lamb in return. I did not want to turn away from him. Instead, because I loved him, I desired to obey him, because I understood that by following him I would know him more. As we spent time together, my thinking and pattern of living were transformed so that I found myself loving what he loved and hating what he hated. By obeying his instructions and believing his promises, I was able to walk on the paths that he set before me．．．paths which drew me closer to him, and not away from him.

Yet, in spite of all this, there were times – like today – that I chose to leave his path and go my own way. And as is always the case, its end was trouble. I was going to have scars from my choices today – scars that I would have never had if I had not chosen to leave the path the Lamb set before me. But, even in this, I experienced the constancy of the Lamb's love for me. He was faithful when I was not. He did not abandon me or cast me aside when I messed up. Instead, when I confessed my sin, he forgave me. That's how steadfast his love for me was.

And his love wasn't just for me. It was for the whole world.

I realized that was why my mission was so important. I had to share this good news with others who had not yet heard so that they could discover the freedom and the love that was available for them if they would believe in the Lamb. If I didn't go, how would they hear? And if they didn't hear how could they believe? And if they didn't believe, how could they ever be free?

An urgency to get going on my mission filled my heart, and I took a few steps, but then I realized I had not explained any of this to the Lamb. I had just started to walk down the path. I turned back to explain, but found the Lamb smiling and nodding his head in agreement with my thoughts.

It was time to get going.

28 - Without Hope

Just as people are destined to die once,
And after that to face judgment...
(Book of Truth – Hebrews 9:27)

The moment I saw her, I knew she was the one that the Lamb had sent me to find.

Tillie.

She sat shackled in chains at the base of a stone stronghold that towered thirty feet into the air. Her clothes were tattered. Maggots covered her rotting flesh. Her eyes glowed with the black darkness that was common in the eyes of the citizens of the Kingdom of Darkness.

From behind a pile of rocks, I watched as she glanced to the left and the right. When no one appeared, she slipped a key out of one of her boots. With a perfected skill, she reached the key into the lock that bound her chains to the wall. Within seconds, she was freed from the wall, but chains still bound her hands and feet. Crouching low, she gathered up her chains, and shuffled quickly across the ground, putting distance between herself and the stone edifice to which she had been fastened.

Her freedom was short lived.

Around the corner of the fortress came two members of the dog-wolf packs that belonged to the Horde, followed by two evil guards. At the sight of the empty space where their captive been, a cry of alarm was raised. The dog-wolves sniffed the ground and picked up her scent. Within moments, they were upon her.

One grabbed hold of her arm and jerked her out of the bush where she hid. She cried out in pain as she was flung from side to side. The other beast lunged at her face. She lifted her other arm to defend against the fangs ready to rip her flesh.

"Hold!"

At the firm order, the dog-wolves released their hold on the girl and took a step back, snarling and baring their fangs. Fed by the hatred and pure evil of their masters, they knew how to strike fear into the hearts of those to whom they were directed to attack.

Once again, they had succeeded.

Her eyes wide with fright and despair, the girl pulled her bleeding arms into her body and huddled close to the ground. The two guards advanced closer as she tried to back up, but the dog-wolves blocked any chance of escape.

"So, you thought you could get away, did you?" mocked the taller of the two guards. He grasped the trailing chains attached to her arms and yanked her to her feet by the arm. "You should know by now that no one escapes from their appointment with Death."

The stubby guard, who had the appearance of a rotund watermelon, rubbed his hands together with dark glee. "Tomorrow we will take you to the Slave Market and feed your flesh to the Scavengers of Death." He grabbed her other arm, and together they drug her towards the stronghold.

"And here we thought we were nice by letting you spend your last night of life under the stars," one of them chuckled wickedly. "Now you will spend your last hours locked in the deepest and darkest of dungeons."

The girl valiantly struggled to get free, but they just laughed and gripped her arms tighter.

Her date with Death was set, and there would be no escape.

Unless she met the Lamb.

29 - Love As I Have Loved You

"...As I have loved you, so you must love one another."
(Book of Truth - John 13:34)

"Wait!" I called as I stepped from my hiding place behind the rocks and tried to formulate a plan. I really had no idea what I was doing. All I knew was that I cared for this girl whose name was Tillie, and I had to share with her the light of the Lamb. To do that, I would need an invitation into the deepest dungeon with her.

"Just a minute," I called out again. The Horde guards stopped, turned in my direction, ~~and~~ They stood there with stunned expressions, ~~with~~ their mouths hanging open. If the sight of their rotting teeth, festering gums, and putrid breathe did not repulse me so, I could have almost laughed, for they did look ridiculous. As I advanced towards them, I marveled at the fact that I felt no fear.

Words from 2. Timothy 1:7 in the Book of Truth filled my mind as I closed the distance between us – *"For the Spirit God gave us does not make us timid, but gives us power, love, and self-discipline."*

The Lamb equipped me with his power for courage, his love to speak with compassion to the hearts of others, and a sound mind trained in his truth so that I could respond to situations as the Lamb would. Armed with these three, I continued forward until I was a few feet away from the trio.

The dog-wolves lunged towards me, but the guards found their voices and commanded them to stop.

"Well, well, well, who are you?" the taller one sneered at me.

"Who am I? I am someone who needs to spend a night in your deepest dungeon," I stated. As the words tumbled out of my mouth, I wondered at how senseless they must sound. Evidently, Tillie thought I was foolish. She stared at me and shook her head, her eyes frantically warning me to flee while I had the chance.

But, the fear that gripped her heart, so evident in her eyes, anchored my feet to the spot where I stood. I would not be leaving. Somehow, I had to share the good news of the Lamb with her so he could rescue her. It seemed the only way I would be able to do that would be from inside the stronghold.

"So, you want to spend the night in our deepest dungeon, do you?" the short, stubby guard mocked as he snatched my arm, and quicker than I could blink, I felt the bite of metal around my wrist. I gasped in pain, as my wounds had not yet completely healed. He laughed maliciously. "That is something we can help you with." As they drove Tillie and me to the stronghold of their headquarters, I was surprised they had not tried to take away my armor and backpack. In fact, they acted like they could not see them.

The building before us towered high into the air. Its circular exterior, built of grey rock, was as smooth as polished marble. At the top, a few of the Horde stood as watchmen on guard. The structure appeared to be without windows or any openings of any sort, except for the exterior doors in front of which we now stood.

Together, Tillie and I were shoved through the doors and into an enclosed hallway that extended ten feet in front of us. Closed doors surrounded us. They were on our right, left, and directly in front of us. The guards opened the doors before us, and we stepped inside of the stronghold. Echoes of misery ricocheted off the grey interior wall, but I could not see where they came from. The inside wall was identical to the exterior — grey, smooth and without windows. There was nothing else inside the fortress. The interior was open to the top.

The guards brutishly pushed us towards a dusty trapdoor. "You two get to see our best accommodations," growled the guard that held my arm. He put a key in the lock and lifted the squeaky door. Before me, steps descended into pitch blackness.

"Get going," he barked, shoving me forwards. I stumbled down the staircase. After three steps the darkness was so black I could not see. Only by putting one foot carefully in front of the other did I make it down those steps without tumbling. How deep we went into the ground, I do not know, but as we descended the air became staler and was flavored with the scent of decay and rot.

Finally, we reached the bottom. The guard released his hold on my arm. I heard him fumbling with another lock, and another door squeaked open. They shoved Tillie and me through a small opening, and I landed on my hands and knees. Behind me, I heard the door screech shut, and cruel laughter as the guards promised to return for us in the morning.

I tried to stand, but my head bumped into the roof of that prison before I was able to stand straight. Hunching, I let my fingers trail over the damp walls, using them to determine the size of the room. I stretched my arms out, and each fingertip touched a side of the cavern.

Cool fingers bumped into mine and gripped my hand tightly before tugging me to the floor. At the sound of small, scampering feet beside me,

I took a shuddering breath before I sat down. Hopefully, I would not make a pancake out of a rat. One advantage of the darkness was that I could not see the vermin that made this dungeon their home.

I hugged my knees to my chest and waited. Now that I was here with Tillie, I was unsure of how to start a conversation. Thankfully, I did not have to wait long for Tillie to speak.

"What are you doing?" she whispered suspiciously. "Why did you come to this place? You were free!"

I paused before I answered. What response could I give? I had witnessed her desire to be free. I saw the fear in her eyes when she was recaptured. I understood only too well the feeling of despair and hopelessness that accompanied the truth that there was nothing that slaves could do on their own to change their destiny with Death.

What had propelled me on this crazy mission into the deepest dungeon?

Love for the Lamb and love for Tillie had. Although I did not know her, compassion for her filled my heart and compelled me to join her where she was so that she could discover the Lamb and the freedom only he could give.

But how did I explain all this to her? At that moment I did not know, so I opted to keep my answer simple. I turned my head in the direction of her voice, and stated, "I came because of you."

30 - The Escape

…He breaks down gates of bronze and cuts through bars of iron.
(Book of Truth – Psalm 107:16)

A bitter laugh filled the darkness. "Me? You came because of me? You don't even know me. Why would you care what happens to me?"

"Because I have been where you are. I know what it is to be bound in chains. I understand the desire ~~of freedom~~ to be free and to live life that burns so deeply within your heart. I have felt the hopelessness that hounds every breath because deep down inside you know that regardless of what you try, there is no escape from your appointment with Death. I have watched countless citizens of the Kingdom of Darkness try to pay the debt owing against them, only to fail and be thrown ~~into~~ through the Gates of Death, never to return. I have heard their cries of utter despair and deep misery on the other side of that wall – cries that never end."

I paused and wiped away the tears that were running down my face. How could I help Tillie understand that death did not have to be her destiny? There was hope – living and vibrant – for her if only she would believe in the Lamb.

Quiet sobs filled the darkness of that chamber, and I reached into my backpack and pulled out the Book of Truth. Its soft, golden light filled that dark chamber. The sweet fragrance of its words of life chased away the scent of death and decay. She crept closer to me, and I began to tell her my story.

I explained how the Lamb had paid my debt and rescued me from death. I told her of the freedom that was suddenly mine when my debt when sailing through the air nevermore to return and the chains that had bound me fell away. I recounted to her of running with the Lamb in the meadows of the Kingdom of Light, discovering that he had loved me before the beginning of time and that his love was always, forever, no matter what. His love for me did not change even when I messed up. Instead of casting me aside, he forgave me and restored to me the joy of a right relationship with him. I showed her the scars on my wrists, knees, and ankles as evidence.

As minutes slipped into hours, words of hope and promise poured out from my heart to hers. Her head nodded in understanding as we read these words in John 3:16 from the Book of Truth – *"For God so loved the world, that he gave his one and only Son, that whoever believes in him shall not perish but have eternal life."*

The light of truth illuminated the darkness of her mind, and there in that deepest dungeon of the stronghold of the Prince of Darkness, we knelt together. With hands raised upwards, she said two simple words filled with hope.

"I believe."

With those two words, blazing light shot forth from the Word of Truth and blasted open the prison door. The chains that bound us snapped. The ground beneath us trembled as dirt and rocks tumbled onto the dungeon floor. We grasped each other's hands and ran to freedom.

When we reached the top of the staircase, the trapdoor was open. In fact, all the doors were wide open. We clambered out of the opening and raced outside to the Lamb. Immediately his love surrounded us.

Yet, while joy radiated from his eyes, I noticed a trail of tears running down his face. I stepped back. "What is it?" I questioned, but before he answered, the dog-wolves were upon us — the whole pack.

Their hideous fangs ripped into our flesh, shredding it until the ground was red with our blood. Our cries of pain mingled with their howls of pleasure as they feasted on our destruction. I struggled to reach Tillie, my friend, but I could not get to her. Then, darkness swallowed me, and I knew no more.

31 - Joy Indescribable

...but the gift of God is eternal life in Christ Jesus our Lord.
(Book of Truth – Romans 6:23)

I lay quietly on the ground. The attack was over. It seemed that the dog-wolves and the Horde had left us. Silence filled the air. As I opened my eyes, all I felt was throbbing pain. I rolled over to see if I could find Tillie.

She lay in a bloodied heap about four feet away. Streams of blood ran down her slashed face, but as she opened her eyes, I saw the light of hope radiate from them.

And she smiled.

I struggled to close the gap between us and managed to reach out and touch her hand.

She motioned upwards and whispered in a voice filled with pain and joy. "Do you see them? They are so beautiful!"

Looking up, I saw that the air was filled with golden light radiating from heavenly beings.

Angels.

Their hands reached down to my friend and lifted her. The blood and the bruises disappeared as joy indescribable filled her face, and she was carried away.

I reached upwards, desiring to go where she was going. Home. Heaven.

"Please," I pleaded. "Take me too."

I watched as the golden beings of light disappeared, and then a shudder of pain radiated through my body. I closed my eyes and once again fell into the blackness.

32 - A Flickering Ember

"In this world you will have trouble.
But take heart! I have overcome the world."
(Book of Truth – John 16:33)

When I awakened an eerie, orange light hovered around me. I struggled to my feet, trying to make sense of where I was. The last memory I had was that of the angels of light carrying Tillie away and leaving me behind. My eyes adjusted to the darkness, and I wished I could fall back into oblivion.

The Horde encircled me. Their hideous forms reflected in the flickering fire beside me. With their talons extended, they lashed at me as they cavorted in a vicious dance of victory around me. With every slash, I writhed in pain. They cut me again and again. Tiny rivers of blood dripped to the ground from my back, shoulders, and arms. The scent and sight of my wounds only increased the frenzy of their assault.

I fell to the ground, too weak to stand. Screeches haunted the air as tears slid down my face. I was so weak. So tired. So weary of trying to keep on. Of hoping. Of holding onto the promises. Of standing.

My eyes closed. The darkness was so black. Cold stiffness settled across my limbs as a black winged creature descended. Even the demonic Hordes lessened their cries as the Beast of Darkness entered the circle where I lay. Sulphuric acid spewed from his nostrils as his cloak of hopelessness and fear enveloped me.

The strength of his darkness was so powerful, the flames of the fire beside me sputtered and then went out. All that remained was a bed of flickering embers. As each one cooled, a trail of smoke, deadly in its beauty, slowly drifted upwards as the last bit of life was extinguished. From outside the fire's jagged circle, a ring of blackness formed as one by one the coals were snuffed out. Finally, all that remained were a few scattered cinders, courageously struggling to stay alive, but within themselves, they were unable to stop the inevitable grip of darkness that would soon envelop them.

In the same way, I felt the ember of my life flicker and sputter. It was faltering, growing smaller. Soon it would be snuffed out. With a final breath, I whispered, "Help."

The cry was so quiet, it was not heard by those who surrounded me, so intent was their gaze on the destruction of my life. I had dared to obey the Lamb and enter their dungeon to rescue a prisoner. They were going to exact their price as brutally as they could.

But then, out of the utter blackness, leaped the Lamb. He entered the circle, glowing in brilliance. Warriors of light accompanied him and took up the battle with the demonic Hordes. Swords slashed the night air. The sound of the clash between light and darkness raged as the Lamb crouched beside me and stared at the winged creature.

"Begone, vile one of hopelessness and despair. Take your Horde with you. This is my beloved, and I will not let her ember be snuffed out." The Lamb spoke with authority. The creature drew his cloak around him and gave an unearthly shriek. He had no choice but to obey. He and the Hordes fled into the blackness of the night.

I lay in the silence, surrounded by the angelic host that formed a garrison of light around me. Even though sweet peace filled the air, I was too weak to move. Dark cold had filled me until the only life left in me was the flickering ember of my heart. But then I felt a breath on me, warm and sweet, and life began to seep into me. I lifted my head and smiled in gratitude to the one who would not allow my flickering ember to be snuffed out.

I fell into a peaceful sleep, garrisoned by the light of the Lamb.

33 – Relief and Rest

The Lord is close to the brokenhearted and
Saves those who are crushed in spirit.
(Book of Truth – Psalm 34:18)

A cool cloth wiped my wounds, bringing sweet relief to the pain the radiated through my body. I opened my eyes and saw the Lamb wiping away the dried blood that caked my wounds.

I looked at him, unable to speak. He gave me a drink. I swallowed painfully, and then whispered, "Tillie?" My mind struggled to catch up with all the events that had taken place. I was not sure what reality was.

"Her life here was done. She has entered the Gates of Life and is at home in heaven where she will know the complete fullness of eternal love, joy, and peace. For her, there will be no more pain. No more tears. No more death. She is home. One day you will join her, but for right now, you need to rest."

The Lamb gave me another drink and a piece of bread to eat. He stayed with me and did not leave. Slowly, my strength returned, and when I could stand, he took me by the hand and said, "Come, follow me."

Together we walked to a place of peace and tranquility so that I could continue to heal and recuperate. I still remember the first time I saw the silver waters washing against the white sand. For a moment the heaviness in my soul lifted as I twirled in the sand and raised my hands to the sky.

"Do you like this place?" the Lamb asked me.

"Oh, yes!" I replied.

"Then here we will stay for a while," he said. "Here, I will give you rest for your soul."

34 - My Restless Soul

"For my thoughts are not your thoughts, neither are your ways my ways," declares the Lord. "As the heavens are higher than the earth, so are my ways higher than your ways and my thoughts than your thoughts."
(Book of Truth – Isaiah 55:8, 9)

Days passed as I spent hours walking through the surf along the seashore. I watched dolphins as they frolicked in the waves of the sea. Warm sunshine filled each day as I walked beside the shimmering waves, tracing the line where sand and surf met with my feet. Slowly, my strength returned.

But, while I was healing on the outside, my heart was not. In the depths, far below the surface of my peaceful smile, my thoughts were churning, and my soul was not at rest. Too many questions about the happenings at the fortress were swirling in the chaos of my mind for my soul to enjoy the peace of the sea.

How could the events of the mission turn out as they did? Had not the Lamb sent me on this mission, even sending me into the abyss of the prison so that I could reach Tillie and she could have life in him? Had not this been his purpose?

Yet, she had not lived. She had died.

As these thoughts tumbled in my mind, more questions arose. Tillie's story had ended so differently than mine. I had thought her journey would have been similar to mine with a trip to the Slave Market where the Lamb would pay her debt. Then, she would have seen her name written in the Lamb's Book of Life, walked through the Narrow Gate and spent days, months and years discovering the joy of knowing the Lamb as she learned to love and follow him.

But, that had not happened. Had I messed up somewhere? Had I made a mistake? Had I misunderstood his instructions? As my mind tossed and turned with these thoughts, I remembered my wayward moment off the path of the Lamb. Had my failure that day caused enough of a delay that I had contributed to her death instead of her life? Had my faults overpowered the Lamb's plan and prevented his purposes from being fulfilled?

Sleepless nights mixed with my unanswered questions created an inferno within me that threatened to erupt. I found it increasingly ~~harder~~ more difficult to keep hidden the storm that was brewing in the thoughts of my restless mind and soul.

Where could I find the answers that I so desperately needed? Could I go to the Lamb? If he answered me, would I be able to bear his answers? What if he told me that I had misunderstood his instructions and it was my fault ~~she~~ Tillie had died as she had? What if he said that it was because of my wayward ways that his plan had been skewed and set off course?

As my thoughts traveled down that path, darkness overwhelmed me. I sank to my knees and held my head in my hands, trying to ~~keep~~ hold in the pressure that was building in my mind and my heart. I loved the Lamb so much. My heart desired to know him more completely so that I would love him more thoroughly and be able to follow him more fully.

But, the simple truth was that I did mess up. I did make mistakes. As much as I wanted to, I didn't always understand the Lamb's will correctly. I struggled to do what was right because honestly, there were times when I desired to do what was wrong. It was like there was a struggle going on in me. The good I wanted to do, I didn't do, and the wrong that I didn't want to do – well, that was the very thing that I ended up doing!

Sobs ripped through my body as all the churning in my heart and mind spilled over.

Who would help me? Who would save me?

In desperation, I looked up and there I saw the Lamb.

35 - Hard Questions

*"As the rain and the snow come down from heaven, and do not return
to it without Watering the earth and making it bud and flourish, so that
it yields seed for the sower and Bread for the eater, so is my word that goes
out from my mouth: It will not return to me empty, but will accomplish
what I desire and achieve the purpose for which I sent it."*

(Book of Truth – Isaiah 55:10, 11)

As the Lamb sat down in the sand beside me, his light ~~filled~~ shattered the
darkness that had enveloped my mind, and I felt hope begin to flicker once
again. If anyone could help me, it would be the Lamb. But, then just as
quickly, a cold gust of fear threatened to puff it out for how could I endure
the answers he might give to my questions?

Timidly, I looked into his eyes, and there I did not see
condemnation or judgment. Instead, I saw his compassion for me, and I
remembered how he had shown me that he loved me. Always. Forever.
No matter what. His love for me was that powerful. That enduring. That
steadfast. Nothing would change it. How could I have forgotten?

As I remembered these truths, the ember of hope flickered brighter. Its warmth warded off the cold wind of fear, and the storm that had been churning inside of me began to still. I looked to the Lamb.

He smiled at me, and in his presence, I took courage. We sat in silence and then he spoke, "For many days you have been troubled by thoughts that have caused you to question many things. Why did you not come to me?"

I shrugged my shoulders. How could I put into words all that had been churning in my mind? Again, I looked at the Lamb. In the light of his truth and patient love for me, the tangled web of my thoughts unraveled to reveal the root from which my churning questions had sprung.

"I was afraid."

The Lamb nodded in his knowing way as he asked a probing, yet simple question, "Why?"

"The mission I undertook ended so differently than I expected. You sent me on this mission to tell Tillie about the good news of you, and if that she believed, then she could have life. But, she didn't live. She died." Tears trailed down my cheeks. "I was afraid that my mistakes had messed up your plans, and that was the reason the mission ended so badly. I was afraid that somehow I had misunderstood or disobeyed your instructions, and that contributed to her death. I even wondered if I had imagined the whole mission, and the steps I took were not steps of faith, but steps rooted in some warped delusion of my mind."

I took a shuddering breath as I struggled to express what I had been feeling.

"I love you so much. I want to know you more. I want to follow after you. The wonder of who you are and your love for me has so captivated and filled me that you have become the desire of my heart. Your love is better than life. As I have been learning to love you and to know you more, I have also been learning how to follow more closely after you."

I looked from the Lamb to the ground. "I honestly believed that I was doing the work you had given me to do and that gave me the courage to carry it out. But, when the mission ended so brutally with Tillie's death – well, I didn't know what to believe anymore. How could her death have been a part of your plan?"

At this, I stopped, and silence filled the air as I finished voicing the turbulent thoughts of my heart. Although my gaze wandered to that place in the distance where the sky met the frolicking waves of the sea, my mind focused on the Lamb.

What would he say?

36 - Braveheart

...Be strong and courageous. Do not be afraid; do not be discouraged,
For the Lord your God will be with you wherever you go.
(Book of Truth – Joshua 1:9)

"Do you know what name I have given you?"

Startled, I swung my gaze back to the Lamb. This was not the response I expected. I unloaded the tough questions with the deep fears of my heart, and the Lamb asked me what my name was? Had he paid any attention to what I said?

"Do you know what name I have given you?" As the Lamb's gaze pierced past my exterior and into my soul, his question registered in my mind. The Lamb had a name for me? Curious, I shook my head.

"In my eyes, you are Braveheart."

If my eyebrows could have popped off my head in surprise, they would have. Braveheart? Me? I laughed in disbelief. Surely the Lamb must be joking. Had I not just disclosed to him my fears? If he had called me Fearful or Frightened Heart, I would have agreed, but Braveheart? Ha! I glanced at the Lamb, expecting him to see him laughing with me, but he wasn't. Instead, he watched me with an earnest expression on his face. It was then that I realized that he was serious. He was telling me the truth.

To him, I was Braveheart.

As my cynical laughter fled, the Lamb continued his thoughts. "I chose you before the creation of this world to be holy and blameless in my sight. I loved you before the beginning of time, and I have been waiting for all eternity for you to be able to know me and discover the depths of my love for you. I stormed the gates of death and defeated the Prince of Darkness by shedding my blood and giving my life for yours so that your debt of sin would be paid when you chose to believe in me. You are mine, and nothing in all creation will be able to separate you from me or my love for you. Your desire to know me, to love me, and to follow after me are the fulfillment of the desires that I planted in your heart. As you have walked with me, they have taken root and are growing into a tree that is firmly rooted by faith in me."

"Know this, Braveheart, my words are truth. No lie is found in me or my words. Therefore, you can trust and believe them to be true – even when you don't understand or things turn out differently than what you expect. Every word that I speak will accomplish exactly what I have planned for it to accomplish. Your mistakes, missteps, and misunderstandings cannot derail, stop, or overpower my ~~purposes~~ plans from being fulfilled, for my purposes cannot be thwarted."

I shook my head in confusion. "But, didn't you tell me that you were sending me on this mission so that Tillie could have life?" The events of that mission vividly replayed themselves in my mind as I continued. "I found Tillie. She was a captive at the enemy fortress. She tried to escape, so the Hordes threw her into the darkest dungeon. They even put me in there with her. I was able to tell her my story and how you saved me, and she chose to believe in you. The prison door opened, and we ran out of that prison cell to freedom. But then, we were met by the dog-wolves of the Horde and –"

Here I paused. My wounds were barely healed. I looked at the fresh battle scars that crisscrossed my arm. I lifted it towards the Lamb. "How could this have been part of your plan? How could Tillie's death have accomplished your purpose for her to live?"

The Lamb's eyes filled with tears. "Oh, Braveheart. Courage is required to take steps of faith and obedience, and even greater courage is needed to trust the results to me. Steps of obedience do not dictate that events will end how you think they should end. It is my plan that will be fulfilled. In the same way, neither will missteps nor misunderstandings derail my purposes from being accomplished."

He touched the scars on my knees and wrists. "Scars can be indicators of mistakes made and missteps taken." Then he touched the scars on my arms that I had received from the dog-wolves and the Horde. "Other scars are the evidence of courageous obedience to walk by faith and trust in me. But regardless of its origin, every scar proves that in all things – the good and the bad, the successes and the mistakes, the steps of faith and steps of fear, the understandable and the perplexing – I am fully working. This means that my intended purposes for your good and my glory will always be accomplished. I redeem your mistakes, redirect your misunderstandings, liberate your pain, and magnify the steps of your faith, love, and obedience to create something amazingly beautiful – the tapestry of your life." The Lamb showed me his scars from the lashes that he had taken as he walked the path set before him which resulted in his death and resurrection. "Sometimes steps of obedience that appear to end in death can be the very steps that result in life."

"You questioned if you took the right steps or if you misunderstood my instructions or if your missteps had derailed my purpose because Tillie died – a result that seems bad. When in reality, the final result of your steps led to a change in her destiny. The day she died was the day her life in this temporary world was going to end, but instead of going through the Gates of Death, she went through the Gates of Life and entered heaven. Your mission accomplished exactly what I intended, and Tillie is alive in heaven today as a result."

As I considered the words of the Lamb, my fingers traced the patterns of the scars on my knees, my wrists, and my arms. What he said was true. Although I had chosen to go off his path during this mission, he had somehow orchestrated the circumstances so that I was still the one who could bring Tillie the message of good news. My mistakes had not and could not derail the purposes of the Lamb. As well, even though the mission had ended drastically different than I expected, it accomplished what the Lamb intended. Right now, Tillie was in Heaven feasting on the delights of eternal life. As I thought about these things, I realized that my task was not to try to control how events turned out. I needed to have faith, follow the Lamb, and trust the results to him.

I took a deep breath and leaned my head against the Lamb. I heard his heart beating, and in my heart of hearts, I asked him for the courage to be who he created me to be.

His Braveheart.

37 – The Test of the Sea

What shall we say in response to this? If God is for us, who can be
Against us? No, in all these things we are more than conquerors
Through him who loved us.
(Book of Truth – Romans 8:31, 37)

Since Tillie's rescue mission, the Lamb has often brought me back to the sea for times of rest, healing, and refreshment. There were times the work He gave me was pleasant; other times it seemed impossibly difficult. Some missions were filled with great delight, while others brought great pain. But with each work that he gave me to carry out, I continually discovered that he had prepared the way for me in advance and was forever faithful to provide what I needed when I needed it.

It was often at the end of these missions that he would bring me to the sea to spend time with him. There we would walk together beside gentle waves that lapped up against the beach. Miles ahead, the horizon of the sand, sea, and sky joined together to form a picture of peace. We would walk for miles, side by side, visiting, laughing, and enjoying each other's presence. Somehow those times always soothed my heart and soul.

As I recall our times by the sea, one instance, ~~in particular~~, stands out in my mind. The day started out calm and ordinary, but that is not the way it ended.

As we had many times before, the Lamb and I strolled along the beach, but this time instead of walking in a straight line toward the horizon, the Lamb's steps slowed and angled towards a pier, to which a small, wooden rowboat was anchored.

As I followed the lamb, my heart lurched. Why were we stopping here? The Lamb knew I was one of those people who preferred to be alongside the sea, but not on it. A minuscule rowboat was not part of my plan, but as the Lamb stopped before it, I began it understand it was part of his.

"My next assignment for you will not be easy," he said. "Yes, I am sending you out in this boat onto the water. Trust me, for this is my good plan for you. Listen carefully to my voice. You will hear me calling you to 'Come.' Do whatever you need to do to keep moving forward and walk *to the opposite shore* with a heart of faith. Keep your thoughts focused on me and my promises for you."

I gulped as uneasiness settled in my stomach. Why couldn't my sea voyage be in a vessel that was hundreds of feet in length, powered by an engine, and captained by a skipper? The wooden boat the Lamb had for me was six feet in length and had two oars. It would be up to me to power it and steer it. As doubts filled my mind, I was reminded that I had been on enough adventures with the Lamb to know that when he pushed me past my abilities and comfort levels into unknown areas, he always provided what I needed.

This journey, though, would take me not only into an unknown area but also onto the surface of the sea. Walking beside the water and floating on it were two different experiences. Yet, while the Lamb had selected a small boat for me, he had also chosen a sunny, warm day. Maybe this mission wouldn't be too difficult or dangerous.

The Lamb stepped onto the pier and anchored the boat while I stepped into it. My breath came in short gasps as my hands clutched the sides and I sat down. The waves gently rocked the boat, and I realized this was it. It was time for me to go. I locked my hands around the oars and started to row away. It took a few minutes to determine how to steer the boat in the direction I wanted it to go, but I eventually figured it out. Once that was settled, I turned the boat out onto the sea and started rowing.

As I left the safety of the pier, the Lamb called out to me, "~~Take heart, Braveheart~~! The path ahead will not be easy, Braveheart. Much will be required, but take heart for much will be provided. Remember that since I am for you, no one will be able to come successfully against you, for I have overcome the prince of this world and all of his power.

With every splash of the oars in the water, I kept repeating the Lamb's instruction to take heart. Take heart. Take heart.

As I turned back for one last look at the beach before it disappeared from sight, I remembered some of the other words he had spoken. Keep moving forward. Walk with a heart of faith. No one can successfully come against you.

As my oars propelled the boat through the water, I wondered, what type of mission had I been sent on?

38 – To Walk on Water

...Then Peter got down out of the boat,
Walked on the water and came to Jesus.
(Book of Truth – Matthew 14:29)

Hours passed, and as the sun dipped below the horizon, the calm sea was no more. A turbulent storm had crept up as dusk blanketed the surface of the water. Now my little vessel bucked up, down, to and fro like a ~~bucking~~ horse trying to keep its balance on a patch of ice. Lightning ripped through the darkness. Thunder boomed in response. I gripped my oars and rowed, trying to move forward as the waters surged around me, but the storm was too strong, and my strength was vanishing like the fading light.

Yet, amid that violent storm, I heard the Lamb call, "Come!"

I was perplexed. How could I obey the Lamb's call to come and his previous instruction to keep moving forward when the boat he gave me no longer carried me forward?

As I ~~contemplated~~ thought on his directions, I realized that he said I – not the boat – needed to move forward. He had also instructed me to walk by faith. I contemplated those words – move forward and walk. Since the

129

Lamb communicated in ways that I could understand, his instructions seemed clear. Believing that resolved obedience was the key to following the instructions he gave, I prepared to step out of the boat and onto the water. As I lifted one foot over the edge, the cloak of fear and doubt that often follows steps of faith descended and filled my mind with thoughts mocking my foolishness for thinking that I could walk on water. Not only that, if this was what the Lamb's will for me, surely he would have chosen a time when the sea was calm and not raging.

Honestly, what I was about to do did seem dangerous and unwise, but, as my hands grasped the Belt of Truth that was buckled firmly around my waist, words from the Book of Truth came to my mind – *When you go through deep waters, I will be with you (Isaiah 43:2a).*

Despite all that I saw around me and the thoughts that were swirling within me, the Lamb's word was the truth upon which I must stand. When he called me to "Come," I needed to come and trust that he would be with me as I went through the deep waters.

I was unsure of what I would find when I placed my foot onto the surging water. Tentatively, I set it down and felt a hard surface – like that of a stone – underneath the waves. Relief coursed through me as I fully stepped out of the boat and stood up. I was standing on the water! But now, what should I do with the boat? Keep hold of it? Drag it behind me? Let it go?

A wave swept over me, and I lifted my hands to shield my face from the pelting fingers of the cold water. Realizing I had lost my grip on the boat, I reached back to take hold of it, but my hand was greeted with empty air. Frantically, I looked for it, and as another bolt of lightning shredded the sky, I saw the boat listing helplessly on its side as it filled with water, and then slipped beneath the surface of the waves.

For a moment I panicked. I was standing on water in the middle of a raging sea without a boat. I could not go back, so I resolved to turn my face forward and take one step. That step was followed by another as my courage grew and I continued to find a firm surface beneath the surging waves each time I set my foot down.

I had been making my way forward for some time when the smell of smoke tinged the air around me. A small, fiery, orange missile sailed past my face, and another went behind me. I heard them sizzle when they hit the water. I felt a sharp thud as another struck my armor. What were these flaming balls? As another hit the water in front of me, I realized that they were flaming arrows.

Seeking to determine where they were coming from, I peered into the distance, and my eyes traced the black outline of a ship silhouetted in an orange glow. A molten sphere with the appearance of glowing lava was on its deck. Shadowy figures seemed to dance before the blazing furnace, before lining up along the edge of the deck. Above their heads flickered miniature red-hot orbs, and then those balls of orange took flight, rapidly growing in size as they flew in my direction.

The darkness between the ship and myself was polka-dotted with fire as the flaming arrows tore through the waves and the rain to land all around me. I raised my Shield of Faith, and in the dark, it glowed like a fiery star. As torrents of arrows continued to attack me, the air seemed to be filled with thoughts of fear and discouragement, but before they could take root in my heart and mind, my shield extinguished them.

As I continued to stand behind my Shield of Faith, I heard the Lamb call to me.

"Come."

Placing my shield to along my right side, as protection I moved forward through the volley of arrows. For some time their intensity increased, and then suddenly, the barrage stopped. In their place, a menacing, ominous sensation crackled through the air. The entire ocean and sky gasped for a huge breath, and then a flash of lightning shredded the darkness. Thunder vibrated the air around me. Back and forth they dueled, with ever-increasing intensity. The bombardment of arrows started again and increased in strength. Waves of water surged up to the sky, folded in half and then hurtled back to the ocean depths, and I was standing in the middle of it.

By the light that glowed from my Shield of Faith, I caught a glimpse of triangular shadows in the water moving towards my feet.

Sharks.

Time and again they came towards me. With jaws open wide they tried to bite through my metal-clad feet, but they could not penetrate the Boots of Peace that protected my feet. As one shark came in for another hit, a flaming arrow struck its head. It writhed back and forth, twisting in pain as black oozed from the wound. I recoiled as the overpowering odor of decay filled the air.

Vultures, attracted by the scent of death, arrived in countless numbers. The storm did not affect their bombardment as they hurtled towards my head. They descended upon me in a flurry, their talons seeking to get past my Helmet of Salvation and Breastplate of Righteousness so they could shred my mind and my heart with thoughts of darkness, evil, lies, and untruths.

My armor held firm, for it had been given to me by the Lamb. My Helmet of Salvation was forged in his death and resurrection. My Breastplate of Righteousness was not formed with my own good deeds. Instead, it was fashioned by the righteousness of the Lamb.

As I took another step forward, another barrage of fiery arrows hit my armor. Sparks glinted off my Breastplate of Righteousness. Amid this overwhelming offensive, I heard the Lamb tell me to come.

I faltered. With the waves crashing, the thunder roaring, and the vultures descending, I wondered if my mind was playing tricks on me? Was I even hearing correctly? In desperation, I cried out for help, for I was finding it challenging to take heart as the Lamb had told me to do. I was struggling to hang onto his promises amid the storm and the battle.

A gentle, white dove flew past and whispered, "Take heart, Braveheart! Do not be discouraged. Do not be dismayed. I am with you. Be bold and courageous."

Refreshed and encouraged by these words of truth, I stepped forward as another bolt of lightning ripped across the sky, and on my left I saw my enemy, the Prince of Darkness, hovering above the water with his sword drawn. His eyes were two black abysses of evil. His lips twisted into a snarl as he opened wide his mouth and roared directly at me. Vibrations of fear assaulted me as thoughts of retreating tried to take hold of me.

But I remembered that by standing in the strength and armor of the Lamb, I could stand firm.

So I stood.

Faster than a flicker, the enemy turned into an angel of light, and for a moment a doorway of calm seas opened beside him. He extended his hand and said, "Come. You are tired. This cannot be what the Lamb has for you. How could he send you into this? Doesn't he control the waves and the sea and the wind? Is it not within his power to make them be still? If he cares so much about you, why doesn't he calm them for you?"

Through the doorway, golden sunlight danced on gentle waves that lapped against a quiet beach. A longing for peace, for stillness, for quiet, and a release from the storm surged through me as he extended his hand, beckoning me to step through.

But then, in front of me, I heard the Lamb's call, "Come."

I resolved to resist the temptation. Immediately the door and light disappeared, and my enemy turned into a serpent. He slithered to me through the storm and whispered dark thoughts. "Did the Lamb really tell you to come this way? In this storm? In this water? Who do you think you are? You can't walk on water."

I drew my Sword of the Spirit. It glowed with pure light and flashed as I pointed it towards the serpent.

"Even though I walk through the valley of the shadow of death I will fear no evil, for he is with me. Yes, the Lamb's calls will take me through storms, through the darkness, but he does not and will not leave me nor forsake me."

The serpent withdrew his head, and I saw his tongue flicker again as he came in for another strike. "If you continue on this path of following the Lamb you will surely die. You will lose all that you hold dear."

My heart throbbed and broke at these words. Pictures flashed through my mind of my family, my friends, my home. With tears streaming down my face I extended my sword, and once again light shot from it.

"For me to live is Christ and to die is gain. All that I have is Christ's and is given by his hand. I came into this world with nothing, and I can take nothing with me when I die. Blessed be the name of the Lord who has given me a living hope through the resurrection of the Lamb from the dead. He is keeping an inheritance for me in heaven, my true home, where he has prepared a place for me. He holds my family in his hands. He is in control of their future, not you. He will not lose any that have been given to him."

The head of the serpent reared back and then shot forward with a speed faster than I could see, as his tongue flicked back and forth, I saw all the failures of my past flashing through my mind.

"How can you call yourself a child of the King? Look at all the times you have fallen short."

The sword in my hand leaped forward, light streaming and flashing in its brilliance.

"If God is for me, who can be against me? He did not spare his son but gave him up for me. Because of his great love, he has removed my sins as far as the east is from the west. I stand in his grace, justified by the blood of the Lamb, forgiven, clothed in his righteousness. The Lamb who died, and more than that, is seated at the right hand of the Great King, is interceding for me. Who is the one who condemns me? No one."

And suddenly the serpent fled from me. The battleship retreated. The sharks drifted away. The vultures withdrew. The thunder and lightning stilled. The waves quieted.

And I heard the call, "Come."

As I took a step the light from my sword pointed the way forward, and I became aware that the Lamb was beside me, holding me up and strengthening me.

As the light grew, the brilliance of his beauty and glory, the faithfulness of himself, and the truth of his promises overwhelmed me.

I fell to my knees at his feet and wept, thanking him for his goodness, for himself, and for his truth.

And then he said, "Arise! I have prepared work for you. I will equip you for works of service. You are my masterpiece, created in myself, to do good works that I have prepared in advance for you to do."

"You will call on me, and I will answer you and show you great and unsearchable things that you do not know. I know the plans that I have for you, plans of good, not evil, and of a hopeful future. Therefore, be strong and of good courage; do not be afraid. Do not be dismayed, for I will be with you wherever you go."

Then he raised me to my feet and said, "Come."

39 – The End and the Beginning

After that, we who are still alive and are left will be caught up together
With them in the clouds to meet the Lord in the air. And so we will
be with the Lord forever…encourage one another with these words.
(Book of Truth – 1. Thessalonians 4:17, 18)

So, my friend, here we are at the end of this journey of mine; the next is about to begin!

The Lamb and I have been talking during this time that I have sought to record for you some of my journey from the Kingdom of Darkness to the Kingdom of Light and the adventures that followed as I walked with the Lamb in his kingdom. While I have only been able to share a fraction of my challenges, I hope that what you have read will encourage you to trust in the one who gave his life for you, because he loves and accepts you.

Always. Forever. No matter what!

Just as he has been with me, he will be with you.

Always. Forever. No matter what!

Just as he has provided for every need that I have had, he will provide for you.

Always. Forever. No matter what!

There is so much more I want to say, but I don't have the time! I have recorded more of my journeys for you, and perhaps someday in the future – if the Lamb so chooses – they will be revealed. But I won't be here to share them in person, for I have just received my summons! It is time for me to go home to heaven. To the Eternal City where I will be with the King of Kings forever and ever! I hope I will see you there!

Oh, they are coming! The angels in brilliant light! Can you hear them? Can you hear their joyful song? Oh, the joy of perfect love! It is so sweet! So beautiful!

Rejoice with me, for I am going home!

Appendix

Definition of Key Characters and Terms

The Great King - God

The Lamb – Jesus Christ

The Prince of Darkness, the Evil Prince – the Devil, Satan

The Hordes – Demons, servants of Satan

The Angels – Heavenly servants of the Great King

The Book of Truth – The Bible